A Cincinnati

Love Story

Sherri Marie

Deron "Killa" Hutchins

Pow! Pow! I wasted no time placing a bullet in each of those fat motherfuckers' head.

"Help me get they fat ass in the van," I told smoke and Dame.

After we tossed both of them in the van, I pulled off. My phone rang, and it was my nigga, G-money.

"What up, bruh? You busy?"

"Yeah, I'm in the middle of something right now." He knew when I said that, it meant I was in the process of killing somebody or getting rid of the evidence.

"Okay, hit me up ASAP, and don't forget."

"Is everything good?"

"Yeah, but I need to tell you something I think you need to hear. It can wait, though."

"Okay, give me about thirty minutes, and I will hit you back."

"Bet."

We disconnected our call, and I pulled down to the Ohio river minutes later. Once we all got out the van, Smoke and Dame grabbed both of they fat ass out the trunk and threw them in the river. Then, we watched as their bodies floated down the river and then sank.

"Damn, them motherfuckers stank," Smoke said as he smelled his shirt. He took his shirt off, leaving only his beater on then tossed his shirt in the back of the van before he got in.

We made our way back to the warehouse so the clean-up crew could clean the van out. I changed my clothes and reloaded my gun. My guns were always fully loaded. Since I was a hit man, I had to be on point at all times, especially when it comes to my work. I had never been caught slipping, and I wasn't trying to. I called G-Money back on the way to my car to see what he had to tell me. What came out his mouth had me beyond pissed. I pulled up to my house twenty minutes later and stormed through the door.

"Takira, where the fuck you at?" I slammed the door behind me.

"Baby, why are you screaming?" she said as she made her way downstairs.

Soon as she approached me, I grabbed her by her neck and slammed her against the wall.

"What the fuck you got on?" I asked angrily as I looked her up and down.

"Clothes."

"You call this clothes, Kira?"

"Yeah, that's what it is, right!" she said sarcastically.

"Oh, you think shit a game?" I asked as I towered over her. I gave her that look, and she already knew I wasn't playing with her ass.

"I'm sorry, Deron, it won't happen again. I don't know why you tripping."

"I'm tripping because my wife is supposed to respect her body."

"You met me dressing like this. What's the problem now?" She rolled her eyes.

"The problem is you my wife. No nigga should see what belongs to me but me. I don't go walking around with my dick out, because, if I did, you would be pissed off."

She sucked her teeth and blew her breath.

"And what I told you about going out without me anyway?"

She shrugged.

"Oh, so you don't know?"

"Yes, Deron, you told me not to go to the club because it was too dangerous out here," she said with an attitude.

"But you did that shit anyway."

"It won't happen again."

"I know it won't. Now take that shit off now! Matter of fact..." I ripped the red too short dress off her ass and threw it on the floor.

"Deron, do you know how much that dress cost?" Kira yelled.

"Nope, and I don't give a fuck."

She rolled her eyes and went upstairs. One thing about me, I don't play about my wife, my money, or my family. Takira knew if I would've caught her ass dressed like that, I would've embarrassed her in front of everybody. She knew that I didn't play them type of games, so I didn't know why she was testing me. If my boy, G, wouldn't have told me he saw her, she would've never said anything. I didn't know why she snuck her ass to the club anyway. She knew I had eyes everywhere and she was bound to get caught no matter where she went.

I took a shower and lay down. Soon as I closed my eyes, I felt Kira sucking my dick. This was her way of telling me she was sorry. Although I was still pissed, I didn't stop her. I needed to release this nut I had built up inside me anyway. I hadn't busted in a couple of days because I had been so busy working.

Kira twirled her tongue around my dick head then bobbed her head up and down.

"Fuck, you sucking that dick." I palmed the back of her head.

Kira spit on my hard pole and stroked it up and down. She was sucking the life out of me, and I was surprised that I was still breathing. I could feel my nut building up, and before I knew it, I had nutted all in her mouth. Takira swallowed it and told me how good it tasted before she took off her bra and panty set that I bought her for Valentine's Day this year. She knew I loved to see her in it.

Takira climbed on top of me and slowly glided down on my pole.

"Umm." She took a deep breath right before she started to ride.

I gripped her waist and beat that pussy from the bottom.

"Ooh, Deron, what you doing to me?" she panted.

"Nothing yet," I replied as I roughly turned over and put her on all fours.

I ram deep into her pussy, causing her to lose her balance and fall flat on her stomach.

"Nah, get that ass up," I demanded as I rip through her walls.

Her pussy gripped my dick, letting me know she was having an orgasm. I slid my dick out and slurped her juices into my mouth. When I was done drinking from her faucet of love, I slid my hard log back in, and it was wetter than before. I gave Takira a couple of more pumps then I released my nut on her round ass.

"Damn, baby, you the best," Takira said as she lay there barely moving.

I went into the bathroom and wet a washcloth. After I cleaned her up, I lay down. She laid her head on my chest, and we both fell asleep.

In the middle of the night, I noticed my wife wasn't in bed. When I got up to look for her, I heard whispers from the bathroom. I stood by the door, trying to make out what my wife was saying, but I couldn't really hear anything. When I burst into the bathroom, my wife was smiling from ear to ear with the phone up to her ear.

"Who the fuck you talking to this late?" I questioned.

Takira tried to hurry and hang the phone up, but I snatched it out of her hand.

"Who the fuck is this?" I asked as I held the phone to my ear. I could hear whoever it was breathing. "Nigga, I'm going to let you know right now, if you fucking with my wife, you better stop while you're ahead.

"Deron, give me my phone now," Kira yelled.

"Yeah, you better keep quiet, hoe ass nigga, because I'm that nigga you don't want to fuck with. Takira snatched the phone out my hand.

"You tripping. I was talking to Princess."

"Stop fucking lying, Takira. You must take me for some type of fool or something."

"I swear I was."

"Call her back then. Make sure you put it on speaker too."

I could tell my wife was lying by how nervous she was. I knew her like the back of my hand.

"Girl, Deron tripping. Who he thought I was, a nigga or something?" Princess said as soon as she picked up the phone.

"See, I told you."

"If it was her, why didn't she say nothing?" I questioned.

"I don't know. Ask her."

"Because I hit mute on my phone, and I didn't realize it. I tried to unmute it, but I made a mistake and hung up," Princess explained without giving me a chance to ask her.

I was lost for words because I had just fooled on my wife for nothing. Something still didn't feel right, though. I didn't know how she pulled that sneaky shit off, but she did. I apologized to my wife and lay back down. For some reason, I didn't feel like she was telling me the truth. Why would she be in the bathroom talking to Princess at five in the morning? What was so important that she had to go in the bathroom? Any other time, she would talk to her in the bedroom all night. Something wasn't right, and if my wife was really talking to another man, the truth was going to come out.

Takira

I loved Deron with all my heart, and he knew I did. We had been together for seven years, and he treated me like a queen. I just hated that he was always gone. Sometimes we got to spend time together, and sometimes we didn't. We barely had sex, but when we did, it was brand new every time. I met Deron when I was working at Outback steak house; I was his waitress. At first, I wasn't going to talk to him because I was involved with someone, but we were on bad terms.

"Hi, can I take you guys' order?" I asked Deron and the other two guys who were with him.

"Let me get a T-bone steak, well done, with a loaded potato and a side salad. Oh, and my dessert will be you."

I ignored him.

His boys laughed.

"You wild, Deron," Smoke stated. "Let me get the same thing."

"And let me get the Outbacker burger and glass of Pepsi," the other dude added.

"What you two want to drink?" I asked Smoke and Deron.

They both said Sprite.

"Okay, your order will be up soon."

For the rest of the night, Deron tried to talk to me, and when he saw that I wasn't interested, he finally stopped. It wasn't his appearance because he was fine as wine. He had my attention, I just didn't let him know that. When they were done eating, I cleaned up their table and collected my tip. I noticed writing on the hundred-dollar bill they left. It read,

When you stop playing hard to get, call me.

His number was written under his note. I smiled because it was so sweet then slid the hundred dollars in my pocket and made my way to the next table.

I didn't hit Deron up for at least a month, because like I said, I was involved with someone. Things had gone sour between my boyfriend and me, and he ended up getting some years in jail. I was still in love with him, but I wasn't about to wait for him. Plus, he had just got caught cheating on me with some ugly chick, so I was happy his ass got locked up. Now she nor I could have him.

"You know Deron going to kill you if he finds out, right?" Princess said as soon as we sat down.

We were out shopping and having lunch in the mall. I was looking for something to wear for my getaway this weekend.

"Yeah, I know, that's why I got to be careful, Princess."

"Careful isn't the word. You better be safe."

"Princess, I know this."

"Why you cheating on Deron anyway? That man loves you to death."

"Because he's never there and he's always out working. He never has time for me. I got needs just like him."

"Wow, you sound selfish as hell." I sucked my teeth because Princess was right. "You knew the type of work he did before you said I do, Takira. You know Deron is nothing to play with. If he finds out that you are fucking another man, he's going to lose it."

"I'm not worried about it because he's not going to find out."

Princess shook her head. "Just remember, if you get caught, you signed your own death certificate."

"Whatever. Can we talk about something else?" I said, changing the subject.

I didn't want to think about what Deron would do to him or me if I got caught. One thing I knew was that I wouldn't see the light of day ever again. I told Deron that I was going out of town with Princess and a couple other girls from college. Deron did give me a side look as if I was lying, but then he told me it was cool. I made sure I told Princess the same story I told Deron so there wouldn't be any slip-ups. I already almost got caught talking to him in the bathroom last night. Thank God Princess was there with my side nigga's friend.

The dude I was sleeping with had told Princess what happened when Deron got on the phone, and Princess took up for me when Deron called back. Thank God she saved me, or I would probably be dead by now. I knew I shouldn't be cheating on my husband, but hell, I had needs too, I got tired of rolling over and finding him not there some nights.

Although Deron treated me well, he lacked in the sex department. Not saying his sex was bad or his dick was little because that's damn sure not the case. My husband had the best sex and head game a wife could ask for. My ex, Tae's sex was good too, that's why I was so crazy about him until he got locked up. I felt bad for cheating on my husband because I knew if he found out, he would be livid. That's why I tried to be careful about what I did. Deron had eyes everywhere, and I wasn't trying to get caught slipping.

Killa

"What's up, Chief?" I greeted my boss when I walked into his office.

"Killa, just the man I need to see." He took a puff from his cigar then set it in the ashtray.

"I got another hit for you, but I don't want you to kill her. I want you to take her to the building up north. Keep her there until I give you further orders." Chief threw a picture down in front of me.

"This her?"

"Yeah."

Damn, she's beautiful, I thought as I folded the picture and stuck it in my pocket.

"Here is some more information about her whereabouts." He handed me a paper with all her information on it.

It had her name, height, weight, job, where she hangs out, and so on. Chief was always on point when it came to shit like this. He was one of the most paid kingpins in the city and pushed all type of weight. He never touched the drugs, though; he had workers for that like Smoke and Dame. Anything you need, Chief had it on the streets. Kush, cocaine, x pills, lean, meth you name it, he supplied it.

I slid the paper with her information on it in my pocket.

"I got a question, Chief."

"What's that?" he asked as he blazed his cigar back up.

"Why you don't want me to kill her?"

"I got my reasons, and right now isn't a good time to talk about it. Get her as soon as possible, and make sure you don't hurt her."

"Okay, I got you."

I got up and made my way out. When I got in the car, I called my wife and told her to get ready because I was taking her out tonight. Lately, we hadn't been spending time together because I had been so busy. I thought it would be nice if I took her out on a date. We usually went on a date every weekend, but we hadn't been on one in about a month.

***

Later that evening, we walked into the restaurant and waited for the waitress to seat us. When we sat down, the waitress took our order. I went to the restroom to wash my hands and then sat back down at the table. My wife didn't even notice me watching her as she stared at her phone with a smile on her face.

"What's got you smiling so hard, baby?" I questioned.

"Oh, nothing. Just something Princes said." She stuck her phone down in her purse and took a sip of her water.

"How was your day?" she asked.

"It was alright," I replied, noticing that my wife had quickly changed the subject. I was going to address it, but I didn't want to ruin the night.

The waitress brought our food, interrupting our conversation. We said our grace and talked over dinner. After we were done eating, we had a couple of drinks.

As we were leaving, I couldn't help but notice some dudes staring in a black Cadillac with tinted windows. The two front windows were halfway down, and the back windows were up.

"You know these niggas?" I asked Takira.

She glanced over at the car "No," she said and got in.

I kept my eyes on them until I made it to my car, and that's when I heard one of them say, "What's up, is it a problem?"

"Shit, is it?" I asked as I walked toward the car with my gun out.

The man on the passenger side put his hands up. "Damn, my nigga, chill out," he stated scared as hell.

"I just want to know is it a problem, because if it is, I damn sho' can solve it," I fired.

"Killa, get in the car," Takira shouted, calling me by my street name.

"Nah, bruh, it ain't no problem," the dude on the passenger side confirmed.

The driver wasn't saying much, but he stared at me the whole time. I guess he saw that killer instinct in my eyes. I knew almost everyone on this side of town, and I had never seen these niggas before. The one on the driver's side did look a little familiar, but I didn't know where from. That was odd because I didn't forget faces. Deciding to let it rest, for now, I got in the car and pulled off.

Takira

Cancun Mexico

"Umm, shit, eat that pussy, baby." I moaned as I moved up and down on King's face in circular motion.

"You like that shit?" King asked as he came up for air.

"I love that shit, baby."

My clit was stiff, and I could feel myself ready to explode. I palmed the back of his head and pushed King's face further into my juices.

"I'm about to cum, baby."

The slurping sounds that King made turned me on even more, and I couldn't wait to feel him inside me. King pushed both my legs behind my head and dived balls deep inside of me, and I was sure that he knocked down every wall I had down. I dug my nails in his chest from the pain. Even though it hurt, it felt so damn good.

"Who pussy is this?" King whispered in my ear.

"Yours, baby."

"It better be." He started to pound my pussy real hard. "I love you, girl."

"I love you too, King," I stated as I kissed and licked all over his neck.

He started to beat the pussy faster and harder. His fast pace let me know he was about to explode.

"Aww, fuck! I'm about to nut," he yelled as he released his warm nut inside me.

King fell flat on me as we both tried to catch our breath. When me and King had sex, it was always magical. I could feel the love in the air. We couldn't get enough of each other. We have sex at least five times a week. Since I hadn't been getting it from Deron lately, I had been fucking King crazy. It seemed that the more time I spent with him, the more feelings I developed.

"You almost got that nigga Killa messed up the other day at the restaurant," King said as he put on his boxers.

I rolled my eyes. "Here you go."

"I'm just saying, I don't appreciate him pulling out his gun and not using it."

"You and I both know Killa will use it."

"Man, fuck dude! He thinks somebody scared of his ass. I will kill his ass and feed him to the wolves."

"Okay, King, that's enough. That is my husband."

"I know who he is and fuck him. You know why I don't like him, so don't act like you don't."

"Okay, I understand that, King, but this weekend is supposed to be about us. I don't want to talk about him."

King got off me "You're right, let's take a shower."

Although King and I were messing around, I didn't like it when he talked about Deron. That was still my husband at the end of the day. Me sleeping with King didn't give him the right to speak on my husband. I came there to enjoy my weekend and spend time with him.

When he talked about Deron, it made me feel guilty for being there. I didn't want to think about my husband right now because what I was doing was wrong. I knew King was doing it out of jealousy; that was obvious. King also had a grudge against Killa for something that happened years ago. I told King he needed to let that shit rest. The past is the past, and he shouldn't live there.

King knew Deron wasn't to be fucked with and would kill him in the blink of an eye. Killa had so much power that he didn't have to kill him because everyone on the squad was a killer. You're probably wondering why I was cheating if I knew my husband was a killer. Honestly, I can't answer that question. I guess I just hoped he never finds out.

See, King and I were never supposed to mess around this long. It was supposed to be a one-night stand, but unfortunately, it didn't work out like that. We fucked once and had been going hard ever since. No matter how hard I tried to leave King alone, something kept driving me back.

After we were done taking a shower, we went shopping and out to eat. Later that night we went to a club and danced the night away.

Killa

"Come down to the strip club, bruh. Today is Dame's birthday," Smoke suggested.

"You know I don't like the club scene."

"Nigga, just come on. You ain't doing shit anyway."

"Alright, I will be down there in a little while."

We disconnected our call, and I went to get in the shower. Smoke knew I wasn't the club type. It drew too much attention, and niggas are thirsty. I tried to keep a low profile as much I could. Since my wife was gone for the weekend, I figured I might as well step out for a while. I wasn't doing nothing anyway but sitting in the house chilling. I put on my fit and made my way to the club.

When I pulled up, the line was wrapped around the building, but I walked straight in. People in the line were mad and complaining because I got in before them. See, I was known in my city, and I could do to that. The bouncers at the front door already knew who I was and how I rolled. I scanned the club to look for Smoke and spotted him and Dame getting a lap dance from one of the strippers. Taking a seat at the table with a couple of the other niggas on Chief's team, I poured some Moet and watched the strippers do their thing.

Strippers didn't really entice, me especially since I had a beautiful wife. Most strippers weren't shit anyway. All they were worried about was money, dick, and drugs. Some dancers stripped for a good cause, and I respected their hustle. The ones who did it just for the hell of it were the ones I didn't respect, but to each his own. As long as it wasn't my wife or family member on that stage, I was good. Smoke and Dame loved the strip club. They were in there every weekend unless we were working. They had smashed at least half the dancers who worked there.

"Happy birthday, family," I said to Dame as he walked up.

"Good looking out, bruh."

"Look at this nasty motherfucker," I said to Dame and pointed at Smoke. He was sucking one of the stripper's titties while she sat on his lap.

Dame burst out laughing "You know Smoke don't give a fuck."

"I bet he'd give a fuck if Laquisha was in here."

Dame chuckled. "Speaking of the devil."

Dame pointed at Laquisha walking through the door with her baby on her hip. We were laughing so hard we couldn't even warn Smoke.

"Oh, so this what the fuck we doing, Smoke?" she yelled at the top of her lungs. "You are letting this hoe breastfeed you.

Laquisha set their son down on the floor. I didn't know who the hell let her in there with a child. If this child got caught in here, they would be closed for good. She'd better hope nobody called children's services on her ass. Laquisha grabbed the stripper by her hair and slammed her to the floor.

"You nasty bitch!" she yelled as she dragged the stripper across the floor by her hair.

Laquisha has no damn room to be calling nobody nasty, I thought. Dame picked Lil Chaz up while Smoke and the security broke up the fight. Soon as they got them apart, Smoke and Laquisha start arguing like a married couple.

"What the fuck you doing in here with my son, bitch? You so damn unfit."

"Bitch? Oh, I'm a bitch now?" Laquisha swung on Smoke and missed.

He smacked the shit out of her "Why you bring my fucking son in here? See, that's why I don't like fucking with your ratchet ass. Go home and be a mama to my son and the rest of your kids." Smoke grabbed her by her arm. "Bring your dumb ass on."

"Get the fuck off me." Quisha snatched away from Smoke. "Give me my damn son," she yelled and snatched him out of Dame's arms. "I hope that nasty pussy, rotten titty, hoe gives you something," she stated and stormed out the door.

Me and Dame were laughing hysterically, and we couldn't stop. I didn't know why Smoke kept messing with her crazy, ratchet ass anyway. I understood they had a baby together, but she was nothing but a hood rat. Laquisha had five kids including Smoke's son and didn't know who none of the baby daddies were. Not to mention the whole Cincinnati had been inside that pussy. I told Smoke he needed to get a DNA test, but he swore up and down he knew Lil Chaz his. That lil boy looked like everybody in the hood of Winton Terrace if you ask me.

"Man, that bitch crazy!" Smoke said when he approached the table.

"You love that crazy bitch."

"I just love the way she sucks this dick." Smoke grabbed his crotch and smirked.

"You just need to find the right woman and settle down," I stated.

"Killa, these hoes ain't shit. You probably got the last good woman on this earth," Smoke responded.

"I'm not settling down until I'm fifty. It's too many fish in the sea, and I got to catch as many as I can get," Dame said.

"You are going fuck around and catch her," I responded.

"Who is her?"

"Herpes, nigga, along with a whole bunch of other shit."

We all burst out laughing.

"Herpes stands for her pussy everybody shit," Smoke said, sounding drunk as hell.

We were laughing so hard that I couldn't catch my damn breath. I swear I loved these lil niggas. They were like my lil brothers.

"Man, fuck you and Smoke. I'm going to get another lap dance." Dame took his drink to the face before him and Smoke went to get a lap dance.

I texted Takira to see how she was doing. Since she'd been out of town, I had only talked to her once. I would've called her, but I knew I wouldn't be able to hear her if I did, so I sent her a text telling her how beautiful she was and how much I missed her. I might be a Killa, but my heart was soft for the ones I loved.

It was 2:00 a.m. and time for me to go.

Dame was sitting at the table half asleep, and Smoke was still was getting lap dances and throwing money at the dancers.

"Ahy, bruh, I'm about to be out." I tapped Dame on his arm.

"Alright, shit me too." Dame stood too his feet.

We dapped it up with a couple the other people and told Smoke we were about to go. Smoke left with us, and so did the rest of the crew. When we got outside, I saw Princess talking to some dude. I couldn't make out who he was, though. Now, I could have sworn my wife said that Princess was going to be with her.

"Hold up, isn't that Princess? I thought she was with Takira in Cancun."

"Yeah, me too."

"I thought you was in Cancun with Takira," I said as soon as I approached Princess. I could tell she was shocked and nervous. She wasn't expecting to see me standing there.

"I-I was going, but I changed my mind at the last minute," Princess stuttered.

"That bitch lying, bruh. She all stuttering and shit," Smoke stated.

I took my gun out the holster and stuck it under Princess' neck. "Let me find out you lying to me. You going to be buried right next to your friend. Y'all lie together y'all die together."

"Killa, I swear I changed my mind, and she went with the other girls."

"I hope you're telling the truth because I have no problem killing your ass."

Princess was turning red, and I could tell she was terrified."

I removed the gun from her face and stuck it back in my holster. When I glanced over at the dude she was with, I noticed it was the dude in the passenger side from the restaurant. Something wasn't right, and I was going to get to the bottom of this. I mugged his hoe ass and told Smoke to come on. That explained why he was looking at me that day at the restaurant. He knew who my wife was and nobody could tell me different.

"Lying ass bitch," Smoke said then trailed behind me.

We got in our cars and went our separate ways. Something was up, and I could feel that shit in the pit of my soul. I glanced at my phone and saw that my wife still hadn't texted back. I dialed her number, but I didn't get an answer. If I didn't have business to handle tomorrow, I would've been on the next flight.

Takira

"What, are you serious?" I asked Princess.

She had just told me that she ran into Deron last night, and he pulled out a gun on her. She was crying and still scared that Deron was going to come after her.

"Yes, he said if he finds out we're lying, he's going to bury us next to each other."

"Shit! Okay, don't panic. I got this covered."

"Takira, you need to leave King alone now. At least for a while until everything calms down."

"Princess, please don't start. I don't need none of your lecturing right now."

"Do you see how serious this is? You know Killa don't play, yet you're still cheating."

"So? What he doesn't know won't hurt him. Stop worrying yourself. We're good. Deron is not going to find out."

"What if he's waiting for you at the airport, and you don't get off the plane with the other girls you're supposed to be with?"

I got quiet for a second because Princess was right. I knew it was a possibility that Deron would show up at the airport. Hell, he would even catch a flight if he had to or use Chief's private jet to fly him.

"Look, I got everything covered. I will talk to you later." I hung up the phone and paced the floor.

I was scared to call my husband, but I knew I had to before he got even more suspicious. I just had to make sure I said the right words and didn't get caught in my lies. My hand slightly shook as I scrolled down to Deron's phone number and called him.

"You can't call or text?" Deron asked soon as he answered the phone.

"Hi to you too, Deron."

"Nah, don't hi me. I texted your ass last night and called you. You just now returning my call. Why is that?"

I sucked my teeth. "I was asleep. Me and the girls had one too many drinks and ended up falling asleep."

"Until one in the afternoon, Takira? You're telling me that not one time did you wake up to check your phone or go to the bathroom?"

"No, I just got up, Deron. I saw that I had five missed calls from you and called you right away," I lied.

I saw when Deron was calling me last night, but I was to busy fucking King's brains out. I intended to call him back, but I was so drunk that I passed out.

"Who is he, Takira?"

"Who is who?"

"That nigga you with!"

My heart raced, but I knew I had to stay calm. Deron was just trying to catch me in a lie, and I wasn't falling for it."

I laughed. "Are you serious right now? You know damn well I'm not with no nigga."

"That's not what Princess said."

I sucked my teeth. "Boy bye, she didn't tell you no stuff like that because she knows I'm not with no man. If you consider Lisa, Trice, and Miah niggas, then yeah, I'm with one."

"Your lil sarcastic ass mouth gon' get you fucked up, Takira. Let me find out another man is tampering with what belongs to me. You and that nigga gon' meet Satan."

"Whatever, Deron."

"Let me hit you back in a minute. I got to handle this business real quick."

"Okay, love you, Deron."

"I love you too."

I set my phone on the nightstand and got in the shower. I felt bad for what I was doing to Deron, and I knew if he caught me, it would be hell to pay. Deron was nobody to play with. When he was mad, no one could stop him or calm him down. Jesus would literally have to get off his throne and drag him. My husband had a good heart, but one thing he didn't play about was disloyalty. If you hurt him, you definitely were going to feel it. If he couldn't get to you, he would get the closest person to you until he finds you.

My husband might be a killer, but one thing about him is he had a soft spot. When he loves, he loves deeply. Deron was one of the most loyal people you will ever meet. Even though a lot of people trust him with their lives, he trusted only me. Sometimes I didn't think he even trusted me to be honest. Deron has had this wall up ever since his mother was murdered. They tried to say that his father did it, but Deron said it's a lie. He knew how much his dad loved his mother. His father had been on the run ever since. Deron said he didn't know if his dad was dead or alive and he hasn't heard from him since that day. He didn't like to talk about it; he preferred to let the past stay in the past.

After I got out the shower, I waited for King to come back. He had to handle some business and would be back in a little while.

Killa

"Isn't that her right there?" Smoke pointed at the girl coming out of the building we were sitting across from.

I glanced at the picture then looked back up at her.

"Yeah, that's her."

"Come on. What are you are waiting for? Let's get her ass."

"Nah, wait. Not right here. I just want to make sure Chief was on point with the locations."

"Chief is always on point," Smoke stated.

"Yeah, true, but I also got to do my own homework. One slip up can get us caught up."

I wasn't going to kidnap her just yet. I needed to make sure everything Chief told me was accurate. Although he was always on point, I had to make sure myself. Plus, Chief didn't want me to kill her, and something wasn't right about that. I was a hit man, not a kidnapper. Why would he want me to kidnap her and not take her out? Some pieces were missing to this puzzle. I had been working for Chief too long not to know that something was off.

We followed the girl as she pulled off. I just wanted to make sure she was going to every spot Chief said she would go. I also wanted to make sure she wasn't going to other places we didn't know about. After I was done doing my homework on her, me and Smoke went to holler at some dude who owed Chief. We parked a couple houses down and walked up to the door.

Smoke kicked the door in, and we heard music coming from upstairs. When we reached the second floor, the bedroom door was halfway open, and the music was blasting. I slowly pushed the door open and put the red beam on the back of the girl's head who was riding him.

Pow!

Her brain splattered, and she fell on top of the dude, Tony, who we were after. Smoke shot the radio up.

"Where the fuck Chief's money at?" Smoke asked.

Tony's old ass lay there with his hands up. "I don't have no money right now."

"I don't want to hear that shit." Smoke let off a round, striking him in the leg.

"Ahh shit!" he yelled.

"I'm going to ask you one more time. Where the money at? When you take from him, you take from my family, nigga."

I held the red beam on his forehead, ready to take him out. See, I wasn't much of a talker unless I had to, and I liked to be in and out. The longer you wait to kill a motherfucker, the more time they have to think of a plan.

"I don't have no money. Please don't hurt me."

"Look, motherfucker. Where the fuck the money at? Either tell, or I'm splattering your brain just like I did your bitch." I gave him my killer look to let him know I wasn't playing.

Toni pointed to the closet, and I told Smoke to go check.

"It's in here, Killa."

"Alright, grab that shit and let's go."

I pulled the trigger and planted a bullet in his head.

Smoke came out with a black duffle bag on his shoulder.

I picked up all the shell casings, and then we left. We went back to the office and gave Chief his money, and he gave me and Smoke thirty thousand a piece for the job. I was tired of working for Chief, honestly, and I was ready to start my business. I had enough money to buy up properties, clubs, strip clubs, anything I want, but I was so addicted to the fast money that it made it hard for me to quit. I was getting old, though, and I was tired of taking people's lives, even though it made me feel good.

After my mother got killed, I didn't care about anything at all. Nobody cared about taking my mother's life, so I don't give a fuck about their life. I told myself if I ever caught the person who killed my mother, I was going to torture them then kill they ass. I remember that day like it was yesterday.

"Grandma, how are you feeling?" I asked as I took a seat next to her bed.

"I'm fine, baby, just tired."

I hated when she said she was tired because it made me feel like she was going to die.

"You just need to get some rest. Did you take your medicine today?"

"Yes, but them damn pills don't work. I will be fine for a while then the pain comes back."

"Maybe you need to ask your doctor for a higher dosage or some different pills."

"Honey, they done changed my medicine more than you change your draws."

We both laughed.

"I'm tired of them treating me like a guinea pig. They not about to be experimenting on me with all these different drugs and shit."

"Well, when I get rich, you won't have to worry about none of that."

"I know, baby. How is your mother?"

"She's good. At the house right now. I'm about to head over there now."

"Okay, tell her to call me later because I'm about to take a nap. I saw she called me earlier, but I was in too much pain to talk."

"Okay, Nana. I love you."

"I love you too, baby. Come give your granny some sugar."

I kissed my na-na on both of her cheeks and made my way out the door. Minutes later, I pulled up to my mother's house. When I walked up to the door, I notice it was kicked off the hinges. I pulled my gun from my side and walked in slowly. That's when I heard two gunshots ring out.

On my way up the stairs, three dudes were coming down. They fired shots at me, we and had a shoot-out in my mother's house. I was grazed on my arm, but that didn't stop me from shooting back. They made it out the back door, and I ran upstairs to check on my mother. She was lying on the floor with two bullet holes in her chest as blood poured out of her mouth.

"Ma!" I yelled as I held her in my arms. "I got you. Don't die on me," I said.

I pulled my phone out my pocket and called 911.

"My mother needs an ambulance now. The address is 19028 Memory Circle. My mother has been shot, hurry the fuck up!"

I hung up the phone and attended to my mother. I took my shirt off and held it over the wound.

"Son, I need you to be strong," she said in a low tone. "Tell your daddy I love him."

"Ma, stop talking like that. You're not going nowhere."

Tears ran down her face. "Tell your father I wouldn't give it to them."

"You wouldn't give them what?"

My mother pointed at the closet.

I glanced over at the closet, and by the time I looked down at my mother again, she was gone.

"Ma, please don't leave me!" I cried. "You can't do this shit to us."

"Sir, let her go. We need to try to revive her," the paramedics said as they rushed through the door.

I moved out the way and let the paramedics do their job. Watching them trying to revive her broke me down.

"What's going on?" my dad asked as he ran into the room. He froze in place when he saw my mother lying on the floor covered in her own blood. "Oh my God, Deb!

What the fuck happened to my wife?" my father cried as he tried to get to her, but the cops pulled him back.

"Sir, you have to let the paramedics do their job."

"It looks like they are doing a poor job. She's not even responding."

The paramedic put my mother on a stretcher and rushed her to University Hospital. Me and my father got in the car and followed them.

"What happened, son?"

I came back from seeing Grandma, and when I got to y'all house, the door was off the hinges. I pulled my gun out and headed upstairs. Next thing I knew, about three niggas ran down the stairs shooting. We shot it out for a while. I got gazed in the arm, but I'm okay. They ran out the back door, and I ran upstairs to Mom. She was lying on the floor with two bullets her chest."

Tears fell down my father's face. I had never in my life seen him cry. "I'm going to kill them motherfuckers."

"Who, Pops?"

I wanted blood for what they did to my mother. All they ass had to die."

"Don't worry about it, son, I got this. I got to do my homework first."

Before I could question my pops about anything else, we were at the hospital. My father pulled in front of the emergency room door and left the car running. We ran into the hospital and asked for my mother. Within minutes, the doctor came out and told us they couldn't save her. That was the day my father lost his mind. He flipped over chairs, tables, and pushed the doctor against the wall.

"Go save my fucking wife." My father hit the doctor in the face, causing him to fall to the ground.

I pulled my pops back and told him to come on once I saw the receptionist calling for security, which was Cincinnati's finest. We hopped in the car, and he pulled off.

"We can't go back to the house tonight. It's too dangerous," my father stated.

Even though I didn't live with my mother and father, I was always there.

"Mom did mention something to me before she passed out?"

"What did she say?"

"She told me to tell you that she wouldn't give it to them. I asked her what she was talking about, and she pointed to the closet. That's all she got to tell me."

"Fuck! That dirty motherfucker betrayed me," my father shouted and hit the steering wheel.

A few minutes later, we pulled up to the Millennium hotel downtown. My father warned the manager not to tell anyone we were there before he tipped him a hundred dollars, and the manager handed him two key cards. When me and my father got into the room, he turned on the television, and his face was all over the news.

"Vegas Hutchins is wanted for the murder of Deborah Hutchings. His wife was shot in the chest earlier today. Deborah died at the scene. Paramedics tried to revive her on the scene and at the hospital, but it was too late. Police found a gun with Vegas' fingerprints on it, and it was missing two bullets. The same two bullets that killed his wife, 50-year-old Deborah Hutchins. If you have any information on Vegas Hutchins whereabouts, please contact crime stoppers," the news anchor stated.

"Shit, they set me up." My father paced the floor with his hands behind his back. "Son, I have to lay low for a while. I can't have any type of contact with you until I know it's safe. I know you need me right now, but if I don't go lay low, you will be visiting me in jail for life."

He grabbed a pen and piece of paper off the table. "Look, this is the code to my safe in the closet. I need you to grab everything out of there and bring it back."

"I don't know where your safe is at, Pops."

"The full body mirror that's in my walk-in closet, you tap it three times with your index finger and knock twice. The mirror will pop open. Type the code in 2-14-19-85.

That's the date me and your mother met. Pack everything up and bring it to me. Make sure you close the safe back and press lock when you're done."

My father handed me the paper with the same information on it.

"Okay, should I go now?"

"No, go first thing in the morning. Make sure you catch a ride there and drive your car back from the house."

"Alright."

The next morning, I got a ride over to my parents' house. I went upstairs, and my mother's blood was still on the carpet. A tear fell from my eye, and I wiped it away. I loved my mother to death, and I hated that she had to leave us so soon. I was only nineteen years old, and even though I was living on my own, I still needed my mother.

She always kept me level headed no matter what. Now that she was gone, I didn't know how I was going to live without her. I still had my grandma, but it was nothing like having your mother. My heart was broken, and I was sure it would never heal.

I went to the walk-in closet and tapped the mirror three times with my index finger and knocked twice. The mirror popped open, and I typed the code into the keypad on the safe. The safe beeped and then popped open.

"Damn, my pops and mother were loaded," I said to myself as I put the cash in the duffle bags along with two passports and two envelopes. I notice the passports had different names.

When I was finished doing everything, I went back to the hotel. I handed my pops the bag, and he emptied everything out on the bed. He counted out two hundred thousand and gave it to me. He then put the money and envelopes back in the duffle bag before he stuck the passports in his back pocket.

"Son, I will talk to you soon. I have to leave. If I don't, I will be in jail soon. This is about to be hard, but I need you to be the man I raised you to be. You have to hold your grandma up because your mother's death is going to tear her apart. Don't worry about paying for the funeral. We took care of that years ago. I paid for my funeral, your mother's, your grandma's, and yours. Deaths are unexpected, and I wanted to make sure no one struggled trying to bury us. All you have to do is go down to Walker funeral home and give them your mother's name. They will pull up her file, and it will show up already paid for. Son, remember, I'm always with you, even if you can't see me."

My father gave me a hug, shook my hand, and then left.

That's was nine years ago, and I still hadn't heard from him. I wondered if he was alive and well all the time. I just hoped he was okay, but knowing my pops, he was good.

The next day

I woke up to Takira punching me in the chest. "Who is this bitch, Deron?"

"What bitch? I know if you put your hands on me again, you're going to get your issue." I wiped the sleep from my eyes and sat on the end of the bed.

"This bitch!" She threw the picture in my face.

I looked down at the picture, and it was the girl I was supposed to kidnap.

"Man, this is nothing but work, Takira. You tripping."

"Am I?"

"Yes, you are," I said as I walked to the bathroom to take a piss.

Takira trailed behind me. She was getting on my nerves, and I was ready to smack the shit out of her.

"I'm tripping, but you got this bitch picture in your pocket."

"Stop going in my shit," I stated as I shook the piss off my dick and flushed the toilet.

"Nigga, I wasn't in your shit! I was washing the clothes because you sure in the hell didn't do it. When I cleaned out your pockets, I found this." Takira picked the picture up and flashed it in my face.

I brushed my teeth and shook my head at her fucking nonsense. "Look, Takira, I told you this is nothing but work. I never met this girl a day in my life."

"Umm hmm, you think I believe that shit."

"You don't have to believe me, but I'm telling you the truth. When have I ever lied to you? I may have cheated on you in the past, but you're my wife now, and I only want you. What part of that don't you get?"

Takira rolled her eyes.

"Why you starting to question my loyalty anyway?"

"Because of the picture."

I walked up to Takira and kissed her. "I love you, Takira."

I picked her up and kissed her on the neck then laid her down on the bed. When I went to unbutton her pants, she stopped me.

"Deron, stop," Takira said and pushed me away from her.

I gave her a cold look because she never turned down my sex or head game.

"What the fuck are you stopping me for?"

"Because I'm on my period."

I laughed because I knew she was lying; I felt it in my bones. I knew my wife's cycle just like I knew her.

"Pull down your pants, Takira."

"No, that's nasty. I'm not about to fuck you while I'm on. Are you crazy?"

"You just went off your period two weeks ago. You think I don't pay attention to my wife? Now pull your pants down," I demanded.

"No! I'm not pulling my pants down."

I stood over Takira with my fist balled up, giving her the coldest look. "Pull your motherfucking pants down now. If you're not lying, do it."

Takira pulled her pants and panties down slowly. Just like I thought, she wasn't on her period.

"Why the fuck you lie to me, huh?"

Takira started crying. "Because I was mad about the picture."

"That's a reason not to satisfy your husband? Huh? Or is it because you been fucking that nigga?"

"I swear, Deron, I haven't been with no one else," she cried.

"Let me find out you lying to me. You and the nigga are going to feel my wrath."

I put on my bulletproof vest and clothes then made sure all my guns were loaded. I always keep four guns on me. Two on each side of my waist. The other two on each leg, and a pocket knife.

"I promise I haven't done anything, Deron. Don't try to flip this on me."

I walked over to Takira and pushed her against the wall. "I don't have to flip shit on your ass. I told you I didn't know that girl and she's part of a job I'm doing. Since you came back from that trip, you have gotten on my last fucking nerve. I should be the one questioning your sneaky ass. You the one sneaking in the bathroom late at night on the phone and going out to the clubs. You are wearing little ass clothes and lying about being on your fucking period. Not to mention you were supposed to be with Princess, but you weren't. The whole time you were out of town, I talked to you twice, bruh. So, don't talk about flipping shit on you when I should be beating your ass."

I turned around to leave, and she grabbed my arm.

"I'm sorry, Deron."

I snatched my arm away from her and left. I was tired of Takira shit. Don't get me wrong, I loved my wife, but I didn't trust her ass right now. I might not have any proof that she's doing something, but I could feel it in my heart that something wasn't right. I just hoped and prayed that I was tripping because if I found out differently, all hell was gon' break loose.

Jada Sheree Lewis

After a long day at work, my feet were killing me, and I couldn't wait to get home. Today was my last day at work before I went on vacation tomorrow, a vacation well needed. Me and my fiancé had been working overtime to pay for our wedding. Even though he told me he would pay for it all, I didn't want to put all that stress on him. I knew I could be very expensive when it comes to things I want. I just loved nice things What woman doesn't?

Anyway, I couldn't wait to spend the rest of my life with him. He was the best man I ever had. Lately, we hadn't been spending a lot of time together because we both had been working hard to come up with the money for our wedding. Tonight, I was supposed to work a double, but instead, I had someone cover my night shift and decided to do a regular eight-hour shift. I wanted to surprise him with a bottle of champagne, dinner, and of course, me for dessert.

I stopped at the store and got everything I needed. When I got home, I pulled the car in the garage so he wouldn't know I was there. I went straight to the kitchen and started dinner. After I put the steaks and baked potatoes in the oven, I made the salad and put it in the refrigerator. Finally, I set the champagne glasses, utensils, and dinner plates on the table. When I was done getting everything together, I went upstairs and took a hot shower. I slipped on my blue satin lace baby doll set, which was one of his favorites and made sure the house was clean and smelling good.

I talked to my friend, Star, for a little while, and by the time I got off the phone, dinner was done, and I prepared our plates. My fiancé had told me that he would be home about nine tonight, and he had no idea I was there. I made sure that I covered the smell of the food by lighting incense and spraying air freshener before I relaxed on the couch and waited for him to pull up. Next thing I knew, I was passed out.

I woke up to a loud boom in the house and jumped off the couch in terror. It was 11:45, and I called my fiancé's phone, but he didn't answer. I grabbed a knife from the kitchen and checked the whole house except for the basement. I called his phone again, but still no answer.

Another bumping noise reached my ear, and I was sure this time it came from the basement. I open the door and tiptoed down the stairs, praying that no one had broken in through the basement door. What I saw when I finally reached the bottom of the stairs made my heart stop. I was speechless, and I couldn't believe my eyes. It felt like I was about to collapse as I watched my soon to be husband make love to some girl on the couch.

"I love you, baby. This my pussy," he growled as he rammed deep into her from the back.

"I love you too, King." She moaned.

"This my pussy, Takira. Fuck, I'm about to nut."

I watched King release inside her, causing me to get sick to my stomach.

"You dirty motherfucker!" I screamed as I charged toward him with the knife.

King grabbed my arm, restraining me from stabbing him.

The girl screamed and jumped off the couch. She grabbed the pillow to cover her body.

"This what the fuck you do when I'm at work, King?" I yelled.

"Baby, chill out. Please, it's not what you think."

"It's not what I think? You just fucked another woman in our house and told her you love her." I bit King in his chest because it was the only weapon I had at the time. He wouldn't let my hand go so could stab his ass.

"Aww fuck!" King grabbed his chest where I bit him and pushed me away, causing me to drop the knife.

I picked the knife up and charged toward the girl, but before I could get to her, King grabbed me.

The girl laughed. "Maybe if you fucked your man right, you wouldn't have to worry about me fucking him." She kissed her hand and blew me a kiss.

That's when I noticed the wedding ring on her finger. This bitch had the nerve to be sleeping with my man, and she was married.

"Put me down, King. I'm about to fuck this hoe up!" I shouted as I tried to get away from him.

King swooped me off my feet and threw me over his shoulder. I bit his back hard as I could, and he dropped me.

I got off the floor. "You know what? You can have his ass. Neither one of you are shit. Bitch, you married and sleeping with my man. I hope both of you bitches rot in hell where you belong."

I stormed upstairs and grabbed my keys off the living room table then hopped in my car and went to my friend, Star's house. I didn't even care that I still had on my lingerie. All I could think about was getting away from King before I killed him and that bitch. My father was exactly right when he said King was no good for me. Now I wish I would have listened. Instead, I argued with my father and chose King over him. I was stupid for doing that, and now I was paying for it.

I couldn't even believe I lost my character back at the house. I was too classy to be arguing with another woman over a man. It was obvious that she was a thot anyway, sleeping with my man when she's married. Somebody needed to teach these mutts how to be classy.

I pulled up to my friend's house and banged on her door. Soon as she opened the door, I fell right into her arms.

"What's wrong, boo?" she asked as she comforted me. "Who did it, Jada, so I can go fuck whoever up."

"King did." I covered Star's pajama shirt in tears and snot.

"What happened?" she asked as she walked me over to the couch to take a seat. Star grab her Kush joint out the ashtray and lit it. "Now, what the fuck happened, Jada, and why are you in lingerie?"

"I caught King cheating." I laid my head on the arm of the couch and cried my eyes out.

Star shook her head as she took a puff from her Kush joint. She got off the couch and went into her closet.

"What the fuck are you crying for? Let's go fuck them up!" she said as she stood there holding a bat and a pocket knife.

"No, Star, they're not even worth it."

"Well, if they are not worth getting their ass whooped, then they not worth you crying over. Now, this is the last time I gon' ask you. Do you want to go whoop they ass or not?"

"No, I don't."

Star threw the bat on the floor and lay the pocket knife on the table. She then picked her cell phone up and dialed a number. I heard King answer.

"What up?"

"What's up my ass? You dirty motherfucker. How dare you hurt my girl like that. I better not see you or that bitch. I'm killing both of y'all on sight." Star hung up the phone and threw it on the table.

Star had been my best friend since elementary days. Her mother and my mother are best friends. Whenever anyone saw Star, nine times out of ten, they were going to see me. Star was crazy, though, and she didn't take shit from anyone. She didn't care who it was. Star would fight whoever, mamas, daddies, uncles, aunts, kids, grandma, grandpas. She felt like you big enough to talk shit then you big enough to get beat up. It didn't matter if you were a kid or not.

I was the classier one, not saying that Star didn't have any class, though. Star knew how to be a lady, but if you pissed her off, she was a straight savage. I was more of the smart mouth one. You know, the one girl who will crush you with her words and make you want to kill her ass? That was me. I could be nice, or I could be an asshole. It depended on you. I wasn't the fighting type, but make no mistake; I *could* fight. Me and Star had a fight with two cousins at the mall about a year ago. We beat them up so badly that people still talk about it over social media. The video still gets shared on Facebook like it was yesterday.

"I can't believe that motherfucker would do you like that. Does he not see what he got? Not too many women would put up with the shit you dealt with from King."

See, this wasn't the first time King had cheated on me. He had cheated with some hood rat from Laura Holmes projects downtown. The girl was supposed to be pregnant by him, but she supposedly had an abortion. I didn't know how true that was, though. I hadn't heard anything else about it, and no babies had popped up on our doorstep.

I wiped the tears from my eyes. "Star, can I crash at your house for tonight? I don't want to go back home."

"Girl, you don't have to ask. Stay as long as you want, baby."

Star poured both of us some red sangria wine, and for the rest of the night, we talked until we both fell asleep.

King

After Jada stormed out the door like a mad woman, me and Takira made love in my bed. I felt bad for hurting Jada, but shit happens. She would come running back like she always did. Don't get me wrong, I loved Jada with all my heart, and I wanted to marry her. I just felt like I didn't have to be committed to any woman until we said I do. At the same time, I wasn't trying to lose her, especially not over Takira.

I loved Takira, but I knew she could never be mine because she was married. Takira had told me so many time that she was going to leave that nigga Killa—well, Deron as she calls him. I had been hearing the same story for months. I knew Takira had no intention of leaving him, so I didn't give a fuck. I just loved fucking her, taking his money, and getting information from her ass.

The day I saw Killa and Takira at the restaurant together I was pissed. Jealousy was all in my blood that day. I wanted to let him know that I was fucking his wife and how good she sucks this dick. The only reason I didn't say nothing was that I knew what type of nigga Killa was. I knew I would've had to kill his ass before he killed me. Killa was nothing to play with out here, and to be honest, I didn't give a fuck. No nigga scared me, I didn't care who it was. If it wasn't Jesus Christ himself, I wasn't backing down.

Killa wasn't the only one who had a lot of street family in the city. My street family was big also. Might not be as big as them, but it was enough to go to war. See, I didn't like that nigga, Killa, and I had my reasons.

Enough about that lame ass nigga, though. After I dropped Takira off back to her car, I started blowing Jada's phone up all night telling her how much I loved her. I didn't want to lose her because I really did love her, I was ready to take it to the next step with her.

I had picked up a nine to five job to help pay for the wedding, or at least that's what Jada thought. She had told me that she was tired of me hustling, so I lied that I found a warehouse job. The truth is, I was addicted to the fast life, and I had no plans to stop. I just told her that I would so she wouldn't be down my back. When Jada thought I was at work, I was really hustling or fucking the life out of Takira's fine ass. Takira was like a job, though, because she dropped stacks off to me when I asked.

If Killa knew his wife was giving me his hard earned money, he would be pissed. I would be pissed if I knew my wife was doing that. I would cut her body into pieces and throw her ass in the Ohio River. Even though Jada was not my wife, I couldn't imagine another man touching her. Jada was my heart, and I was hers. She was mad right now, but she would forgive me soon. I knew exactly what to do to get her back on my team. She would be making love to me by tomorrow morning.

Killa

I hadn't said much to my wife since I came home. The shit she pulled earlier had me looking at her sideways. I couldn't trust her as far as I could throw her. The past few months had been busy, and I hadn't been showing my wife much attention. It wasn't like I was out cheating or anything, though. That's why I had been showering her with gifts and taking her on dates. I knew the importance of being a husband to my wife. At the same time, though, money still needed to be made. I had a family to take of care of.

Not only did I take care of my household, but I paid all my grandma's bills too. Not to mention I paid for two nurses to be with my grandma. I also paid them extra to do anything she wanted. I didn't care if it was taking her shopping, out to eat, or whatever. My grandma had been doing much better since I got her the best doctor in the city of Cincinnati. She was moving around like a twenty-two-year-old, as she said.

I laughed just thinking about my little old lady. I was going to make my way to go see her today since I hadn't seen her in a couple of weeks. Usually, I went to visit her at least three to four times a week. I had been so busy, though, that I hadn't had the time. I talked to my granny almost every day, though. She had the nerve to tell me she wanted to go to the beach in a bikini. I laughed so hard at her because she thought she was young for real.

"So, you not going to say nothing to me?" Takira stood in front of the television with her arms crossed.

"Move out my way. Don't you see me trying to watch boxing?"

She snatched the remote off my lap and turned the TV off.

"Are you going to talk now?"

"Why did you do that? I was just about to watch him knock that nigga out." I shook my head because she was zoning me out already.

"Deron, I love you. I don't like it when you aren't talking to me. You know that drives me crazy."

Takira walked over to me and sat on my lap facing me. She tried to kiss me, but I turned my head.

"Why are you acting like that, Deron?"

"The same reason you were acting like that with your pussy earlier. You didn't want me to touch you, so why you feel it's okay to touch me?"

She sucked her teeth and turned my face toward hers. "Deron Hutchins, I love you. I will never hurt you."

Takira kissed me on the lips then made her way down to my neck. She kissed from my neck down my chest. She then took off my basketball shorts and boxers. Takira took hard dick into her mouth and licked all over it like it was her favorite lollipop. Once she got me rock hard, she spit on it and slurped it off. Next, she stroked my dick up and down as she licked my balls. She took both of my balls into her wet mouth, and the next thing I knew, she was deep throating me.

"Ooh, this dick tastes good," she said as she stared into my eyes.

My manhood was covered in saliva. Watching it drip from her mouth onto my pole turned me on even more. Although my wife was giving me some exclusive head, I still wasn't about to fuck her ass.

"Suck that dick like you own it," I stated as I pushed my dick deep in her throat, causing her to gag.

Takira pulled me off the couch and pushed me against the wall. She got on her knees and wrapped both hands around my monster. As she sucked, she jacked it at the same time. I look down at her while she gazed up at me. I laid my head back on the wall and close my eyes. It felt so good, I knew it was only a matter of time before I bust everywhere.

"Damn, you sucking the fuck out that dick. I'm about nut."

Takira removed my dick from her mouth and let me release my babies all on her face. I pulled my shorts and boxers up then turned boxing back on and continued to watch it.

"Really, Deron?" Takira said with an attitude.

"What?" I looked at her as if I didn't know what she was talking about.

"You're not going to fuck me?"

"I thought you was on your period."

Takira rolled her eyes and stormed out my man cave. I laughed so hard at her ass.

Takira

I knew Deron was mad at me from earlier, but he didn't have to keep acting like that. At the end of the day, I was still his wife. After I got caught up with King's girlfriend today, I told King we had to stop seeing each other for a while. I couldn't chance anything getting back to my husband. I wasn't leaving King alone for good, just for a couple of days or weeks. We both needed to get our relationships back on track before we lost the ones we loved.

I didn't want to lose Deron because he was all I had. When I met him, I was working as a waitress and barely making ends meet. I lived in a one-bedroom apartment in Avondale. At the time, I had a boyfriend named Tae, but he didn't work. He hustled and spent his money on liquor and weed. If I asked him for money, he would look out for me from time to time.

That's why I didn't want to lose Deron. I couldn't see myself living back in the hood, in that small ass one-bedroom apartment. I had it made living with Deron. We had a five-bedroom house, two car garage, pool, built in jacuzzi inside and outside. Not to mention the BMW, Mercedes, and Range Rover we had parked in the drive way. I was living my best life, and I wasn't about to mess it for King's ass.

Here lately, I had been fucking up a lot, and I could admit to it. That's why I was about to do what I had to do to fix it. King would not see me until my husband was back happy. I hoped King could make it right with his girl because she was pretty pissed when she left, but who can blame her? If I caught Deron making love to a bitch in my house, murder would be the case.

When his girlfriend busted us, I was nervous. She had a knife in her hand, and I didn't know which one of us she was about to cut up first. I kind of felt bad for her, honestly, but that still won't stop me from fucking her man. She was cute, and I could have sworn I'd seen her somewhere recently. I just couldn't remember where. I was so drunk that night that I couldn't remember if I wanted to.

After King's girlfriend stormed out the door, King made love to me in their bed. I wasn't going to do it, but once King started eating my pussy, I couldn't resist. Before King dropped me off, I told him what was going on between me and Deron. Of course, he told me to leave him and marry a real nigga. I laughed because he had just got caught cheating and was talking about he real. Honestly, I probably would marry King if I wasn't married. His sex is off the chain and the tongue is even better. I loved the way we spend time together and have fun. Deron and I used to be like that before he started working late. I knew it was selfish because he was making money to provide for us. I guess I wanted to have my cake and eat it too.

After I finished giving my husband head, I went upstairs and lay across the bed. Princess had texted me and asked if I was coming out tonight. I told her I was chilling at home tonight. Plus, Deron was home, and I knew how he felt about me going out. When Deron was working, I would sneak out to the club more than often. I was surprised nobody he knew had caught me except for G that one time.

Yawning, I turned on a movie and lay there until I fell asleep.

Jada

It's been a couple of days, and I still hadn't talked to King. He had been blowing my phone up and texting me crazy. I didn't want anything to do with him. He had betrayed me for the last time. After what we went through the last time, I would think that he wouldn't be that stupid to make the same mistake, but I was wrong; he did it anyway. I loved that man and couldn't wait to marry him, but after what he did, I won't be walking down the aisle.

I couldn't say that I didn't love King because I did. Love doesn't go away overnight, and I knew it would take some time for me to heal. If I stayed away from King, the healing process would go a little quicker. I got a hotel room at the Embassy Suites in Blue Ash. I had Star put the room in her name, so King wouldn't find me.

Star was coming to join me for happy hour at the hotel, so I got up and took a shower. The drinks were free from 5:30 p.m. to 7:30 p.m., and I needed every drink they had on the menu. That seemed like the only thing that was helping me cope besides prayer. Minutes later, Star knocked on the door, and we made our way downstairs to happy hour. I got two Sex on the Beach, and Star got two Blue Motherfuckers, a drink she knew she didn't need.

"Have you talk to King?"

"No. I'm really done with him, Star."

"That's what you say now, Jada. This break up is still fresh."

"Yeah, I know, but I don't think I can ever get over the fact that he cheated on me again. Not only did he cheat, but he brought the girl into our home. They weren't just having sex. King was making love to her." I could feel my tears trying to form, but I held them back.

"Well, I'm going to keep it real with you. You deserve better, Takira. You're beautiful, sweet, hard working, and any man would die to have you. King is a street nigga, and that's what they do. Not all of them, but the majority of them." Star took her first drink to the face. "Ooh, that shit strong."

We both laughed.

"You're right."

"All you have to do is a give a nigga a taste of his own medicine. I bet he gets his shit together then."

"How am I supposed to do that? Talk to someone else?"

Star laughed. "Girl, did I teach you anything? This is what you do. You find someone you attracted to, right?"

I nodded.

"Put you on something sexy and hit record on the camcorder. Then you ride and suck the shit out that motherfucker dick, then send it to King." We both burst out laughing.

I shook my head. "I don't know why I asked your crazy ass." I was laughing so hard. The crazy part is Star was so serious.

"I'm telling you, the best revenge ever."

"I'm not doing that." I giggled.

"Suit yourself. Let's finish these drinks. I need to go outside and smoke this Kush."

"Okay."

After we were done drinking, we went outside and sat in Star's car. My phone rang, and it was King. I rolled my eyes and threw my phone down on my lap.

"That must be King," Star said and took a pull from her joint.

"Yes, I don't want nothing to do with him."

"Answer it."

"No, I'm not answering him." I said with an attitude.

Star grabbed my phone off my lap, but by the time she was about to answer it, King had hung up.

"Give me my phone." I tried to reach for it, but Star wouldn't give it to me. I could do nothing but laugh at her childish ass. "I don't want to talk to him."

"I know. I'm just about to give him a taste of his own medicine," Star said as she filled her lungs with Kush smoke.

"How you going to do that, Star?"

"You will see."

The phone rang again, and it was King.

"Watch this." Star pressed answer and put it on speaker.

"Umm shit, eat that pussy, Daddy." Star moaned in a low tone so King wouldn't recognize her voice.

"What the fuck!" King shouted.

"Ooh, right there. You about to make me cum. Umm, baby."

I was laughing so hard that I had to cover mouth."

"Ahy, what the fuck! Jada?" King shouted.

Star started to make slurping sounds as if she was the person pleasing my pussy.

"Ooh, like that, daddy. You are eating the shit out that pussy. Umm, umm, I'm about cum, baby."

Star made more slurping sound effects, and by this time, I was on the passenger side floor dying laughing. I couldn't catch my breath I was laughing so hard. I was surprised I didn't piss on myself.

"Here it comes, baby. Aww, fuck. Baby, you the best. Umm."

"Hello, Jada! I'm going kill her ass!" he shouted.

Star disconnected the call and burst out laughing "You heard that nigga voice? He was salty as hell. Now that's how you give a nigga a taste of his own medicine."

Killa

"Man bring your ass on," I yelled from the car window.

Smoke and Laquisha were outside fighting like two big ass kids.

"Fuck you! You nasty bitch!" Smoke shouted.

"Fuck you, nigga! You little dick motherfucker."

"Bitch, you don't be saying that when my dick is in the back of your throat, do you? Nah, you don't. You be swallowing that shit. You kill me acting like you so innocent. I should've left your ass when I caught you fucking that nigga. You lucky he got away, or he would've been a dead man."

"You always bringing up old shit, Smoke! That don't give you the right to fuck my best friend." Laquisha swung on Smoke and hit him in the face.

I could do nothing but sit back and laugh. I knew it was only a matter of time before Smoke beat her ass. Don't get me wrong, I don't approve of a man beating on a woman, but Laquisha deserved that shit.

"Man, I didn't fuck your best friend. Your best friend fucked me! Know the difference. That pissed Laquisha off even more. "I should've been left your ass like my niggas said."

"Who, Killa and Dame weak ass? or Rodriquez and Tone? Fuck all them lames!" Laquisha said and gave me the middle finger. I gave her the finger right back.

She was lucky she was Smoke's girl, or I would've shot her ass. Nobody disrespects me and get away with that shit.

"Don't none of they ass need to say nothing about nothing. All they girls be cheating. Killa's bitch too! fuck you mean. If you need to leave me, they need to leave they no good bitches too."

When Laquisha said that, I felt some type of way. I knew she was ratchet as hell, but why would she lie about some shit like that? I mean, she could be saying the shit out of anger. The way my wife been acting lately, though, had me second guessing if the shit was true.

Man, shut the fuck up. You talk to much! Always running your mouth. That's why I'm leaving your ratchet, loose booty ass, bitch."

Smoke started to walk toward the car then Laquisha jumped on his back and started punching him.

"Bitch, get the fuck off me!" Smoke shook her off his back, and she fell to the ground.

"That's why I'm going to tell the police everything about your ass."

Smoke stopped in his tracks and walked toward her. He picked her up by her throat and threw her on somebody's car.

"Bitch, what you say?" Smoke pulled his Glock off the side of his pants and held it to her temple. "Say what you said again." He cocked his gun. "If you ever in your fucking life threaten me with the police again, I will put a bullet through your skull, bitch! You ought to be happy that a nigga taking care of you and them raggedy, snotty nose kids that ain't mine."

"Hey, Smoke. Chill out, bruh," I said out the window.

The whole Over the Rhine was watching, and we didn't need that type of attention right now.

"You understand me?"

Laquisha rolled her eyes. "Yes, I understand, but—"

"But my ass. Now take your ass in the house and be a mother before they won't have one."

Smoke stepped back, and Laquisha stormed in the house and slammed the door. Once she was inside, he got in the car. That bitch Laquisha didn't have any respect. If she would've told me she was calling the police on me, I would've offed that bitch right there. See, hoes like her you can't trust. Those are the same ones who smile in your face and set your ass up at the same time.

I just hoped Smoke comes to his senses soon and leave her dirty ass alone. I understood they had a baby together, but fuck that. I couldn't do it. I would have to get custody of my baby and bounce on her dumb ass. Smoke was more stable than her anyway. He had a decked out condo, two cars, and money. She didn't have shit but a low-income apartment and five kids. She didn't work, clean, cook, or take care of her kids. At least get a job so you and your kids can get a better life, but she didn't look at it like that. All she wanted to do was fuck, fight, smoke weed, and drink beer all day.

"You good, bruh?" I asked Smoke.

"Yeah, I'm good. I'm about to leave that bitch alone. I'm salty I even nutted in her ass."

"How you know that's your baby?"

"Because that lil nigga looks dead on like me, and he looks like my baby pictures."

"Nigga, do you watch Maury?" We both chuckled.

Smoke emptied the tobacco from his cigar and replaced it with Kush.

"Hell yeah, I watch Maury, but I'm sure that's my son."

"Look, I'm not saying he isn't your son. All I'm saying is be on the safe side. She doesn't even know who none of her other kids' father is."

Smoke took a long pull from his joint, and I could tell he was thinking.

"You're right, I might just do that."

"Alright, let me know what's up."

"Bet."

"You ready to go handle this business?" I asked.

"Yeah, you already know. You got the location?"

"Yeah."

"Alright."

Twenty minutes later, we pulled up to the location. I pulled my ski mask over my face, and Smoke did the same.

Jada

"Look now he really blowing my phone up." I showed Star my phone.

"He will be alright. Now he knows how it feels." Star took a pull from her Kush and blew it in my face.

I waved the smoke out my face and started coughing. "Ewe! That shit stank."

Star chuckled. "Girl, bye, this the best smell in the world."

"Hurry up because I want to go in and get some more drink before happy hour is over."

"Okay."

Star took a couple more puffs of her joint then put it out in the ashtray.

"You happy now." Star said as we got out the car.

Before we could shut the door, we both had guns pointed in our face.

"Oh shit." Star tried to run, but dude snatched her up and threw her over his shoulder. She was punching and fighting dude. "Chill before I pop your dumb ass," Dude stated right before throwing Star in back of the van.

"Get in the van," Dude said, still pointing the gun at me.

"This what yawl weak niggas do, rob and kidnap females? How would you feel if somebody did that to your mama?"

Those words must have pissed him off. Next thing I knew, he picked me up roughly and threw me over his shoulder. I bit him on his back and started kicking.

"Fuck! This bitch bit me!" he yelled as he tossed me in back of the van.

The other dude poured some type of liquid on a white washcloth and put it over Star's nose. Seconds later, she was passed out.

"Oh my God, Star! What did you do to her, you stupid motherfucker?" I swung, and dude dodged it.

He grabbed me and put the washcloth over my nose. Next thing I knew, I was passed out.

When I finally woke up, I was lying in a bed. I glanced around the room, and it was luxurious as hell. Chandeliers hung from the ceiling, and the the carpet was plush. I had to blink to make sure I wasn't dreaming. At first, I thought I was in heaven until I realized I was still alive. I sat on the edge of the bed and held my head because it was pounding. When I stood up, my bare feet sank into the cocaine white plush carpet. I felt dizzy and thought I was about to pass out. I walked over to the door and turned the door knob, but it wouldn't open.

I banged on the door. "Help me! Somebody help me, please."

Seconds later, the door opened, and a dude walked in. He stood about 6'2" with light brown eyes. He had caramel skin, and it was smooth as a baby's ass. His arms, chest, and neck were covered in tattoos. He had a tattoo that covered his neck that read *Killa*. A picture of a woman's face adorned his right arm with a bible scripture under it. The rest of the tattoo, I couldn't make out because there were so many of them.

"What do you want from me?" I asked as I took a couple of steps back.

"Nothing."

"Well, why you got me here then?"

"Because it's my job, that's why. Any more questions?" he asked as he stared at me.

This man was fine as hell, and I couldn't help but notice the wedding band on his finger. Who would marry a man who goes around kidnapping women? Then, I thought about Star.

"Oh my God, where is my friend Star?" I asked.

"She's good."

"She better be. If y'all hurt her, I swear to God I will kill y'all."

"I think you better watch what you say, Ms. Lady." He towered over me, giving me a look that let me know he wasn't playing.

"I will be back to check on you later. You hungry?"

"No. I don't want none of your nasty ass food."

He shook his head and laughed then made his way out the door.

Killa

When I arrived home, I was happy to see that Takira's car wasn't there. I didn't want to see her or talk to her. That bullshit she pulled the other day still had me heated. I got in the shower, and by the time I was done, I heard Takira's voice.

"Babe?" she called out as she walked into the bathroom.

I turned the shower off and grabbed my dry off towel.

"What's up, Takira?" I said with an attitude as I dried off and wrapped the towel around my waist. I didn't even want her in my presence.

"Baby, you still mad at me?" she tried to kiss me, but I moved away. "Why are you acting like that, Deron?"

"The same reason you're acting like that," I stated as I made my way out the bathroom.

"Oh, hell nah," Takira yelled and pushed me.

"Is you mother fucking crazy? Don't ever put your hands on me, Takira. What I tell you abut that?"

"What bitch bit you on your back?"

Damn, I didn't even know how I was about to explain this because she wasn't going to believe me anyway. Even though it was nothing, Takira would make it something like always.

"Man, that shit happened at work," I explained as I put my clothes on.

"You a damn lie, Killa. What they do, bite you before you killed them?"

"Here you go, man. I don't have to explain shit to you. I told you what happened."

"Fuck you, Deron!" Takira threw her purse at me and missed. Everything in her purse flew out when it hit the floor.

She ran over to pick everything up, and I couldn't help but notice how fast she was trying to stuff everything in her purse. I snatched the purse out her hand and emptied it out on the bed.

"Give me my purse." Takira tried to fight me for it, but I pushed her little ass back.

I unfolded the paper, and it was the hotel receipt from Cancun Mexico. I scanned the paper, only to see two guests and one king sized bed. If my wife went with several other girls, why would she get one bed? Plus, it said two guests, so why wouldn't she get two beds was the question.

"Who the fuck was you at the hotel with, Takira?" I asked as I faced her.

"I told you who I was with, Deron. Why are you tripping?"

"You must think I'm some type of fool or lame out here. Why you keep playing with me, bruh?" I asked as I looked into her eyes. I could tell my wife was hiding something because she had guilt all over her face.

"I know you're not a fool, baby, but you got to believe me. I'm not cheating."

Before I knew it, I smacked the shit out of her "Who the fuck is he? Because I'm going to kill your ass and his."

"Deron, I can't believe you hit me," she said as she held her face.

I grabbed her off the floor and pinned her against the wall.

"You think I give a fuck about them tears, Takira, huh? Tell me who that nigga is, or I'm going to beat your ass."

"Baby, I swear it isn't no one else. We decided to get one bed because two was too expensive."

I laughed because when did she ever care about how much shit cost? Takira was going to tell me the truth, even if I had to beat it out of her. I wasn't going to kill her until I found out the truth, but I knew she wasn't going to tell me. A part of me wanted to believe my wife, but the other part told me not to. I pulled my gun off my waist and stuck it in her mouth.

"I will kill your ass right here and not give a fuck." I cocked my gun. "Now, who the fuck were you with?" I removed the gun from her mouth so she could talk.

"Nobody but the girls. I swear," she sobbed.

I shook my head. "When I married you, I married you because I loved you. You were one of the realest females I ever met. Now I don't know how to look at your grimy ass. Let me find out you're lying, and another man had what belongs to me. I'm going to make sure I make you suffer."

I put some clothes in the duffle bag and left. Takira trailed behind me trying to beg me to stay, but I didn't even acknowledge her ass. I wasn't about to play these games with my wife. Since Takira wanted to play these fucking games, I had something for her ass. I was going to make her feel it one way or another.

A little while later, I made it back to the house in Indian Hills where we were keeping the girls. I put my belongings in the room I was staying in and went to check on Jada.

"You good?" I asked soon as I walked in the door.

She was sitting in the middle of the bed crying her eyes out. I felt bad, honestly, but this was part of my job.

"Do I look good to you?"

Honestly, yes you do. You look good as hell." I smiled.

Jada was pretty as hell. She was light skinned with long, black hair that went to the middle of her back. She had pretty brown eyes. If they were a shade lighter, they would've been hazel. She stood about 5'2", and she was thick in all the right places.

"Whatever, smart ass." She rolled her eyes.

"You hungry yet? I got some pizza."

"No, fuck that food. I want to go home. Why you got me here anyway?" she asked with her arms folded across her chest.

"You will find out soon."

"How soon is soon? I don't have time for this shit. I do have a life, and it don't consist of kidnapping people either," she fired.

I laughed. "You got a smart ass mouth."

"You think?" she asked sarcastically.

"That rude ass mouth was going to get your little ass fucked up. For you to be so little and cute, you talk a lot of shit. I hope you can back that shit up," I stated and walked out the door not giving her time to reply.

Takira

"He doesn't love me anymore," I said as I cried my eyes out on Princess' shoulder.

"Yes, he does. He's just upset right now, Takira."

"I fucked up. I should've listened to you."

I knew Princess wanted to be like, *I told you so*, but this wasn't the right time.

"Don't beat yourself up about it. He doesn't have any proof. He's just assuming, Takira."

I wiped the tears away from my face. You're right, I'm tripping. I know Deron loves me. I've just never seen him act like that. When he put that gun in my mouth, I just knew my life was over."

"You know what you have to do now."

"What's that?"

"You got to let King go."

"I know. Me and King haven't seen each other in a couple of days. I didn't tell you that his girlfriend walked in the basement and caught us fucking."

"What? Oh my God."

"I know right."

"What happened?"

I told Princess the story of how everything went down. When I was done filling her in, all she could do was shake her head. Princess had warned me plenty of times to leave King alone, but I didn't listen. I wanted to have my cake and eat it too. If I could have ice cream with it, I would. I had been blowing Deron up since he left, but he hadn't returned any of my calls or text messages.

It wasn't like Deron to act like this. We had our problems, but we always seemed to work them out no matter what. I didn't know what the hell had gotten into Deron. I knew he was mad because I lied about being on my period that day and about the hotel receipt. That still didn't prove that I was cheating. Although I was, he didn't have no proof.

What made me mad was that his ass had a bite mark on his back. I wondered what bitch did that because no man was about to bite another man unless they were gay, and I knew Deron wasn't around any gay men. Maybe that was why Deron keep accusing me of cheating. Maybe it was really him. He was trying to blame everything on me to cover his ass. That's why his attitude had changed toward me lately. It wasn't me, it's him doing the dirt. I knew one thing; I better not catch him with no other chick, or he was going to see me act a fool.

For the majority of the day, I stayed at Princess' house. I told her about how I found a bite mark on Deron's back. She didn't believe that he would cheat on me or do anything to hurt me. She could be right, but I still wanted to know how in the hell the bite mark got there.

I decided to spend the night at Princess' house. I didn't want to go home knowing that my husband wouldn't be lying next to me. It hadn't even been twenty-four hours yet, and I missed him so much. I wasn't used to Deron being mad at me. I picked up the phone and dialed his number again, but I still didn't get an answer, so I sent him a good night text and told him I loved him.

All I wanted to do was lie in his arms and talk the situation out. I loved my husband, and I didn't want to lose him. Plus, I couldn't see him with another woman besides me. Deron was such a good man despite the fact that he takes people's life. He gave me everything I wanted and more. I guess when you want to have your cake and eat it to, you must pay the consequences.

I lay down on the couch and scrolled through my Facebook page. I was bored out my mind. Princess had fallen asleep on me an hour ago, and I was just up thinking. After I was done going through my Facebook page, I texted Deron one more time to let him know he was on my mind. I lay there until my eyes got heavy, and then I finally fell asleep.

Killa

"Hey Na-Na how you been?" I gave my grandma a kiss on the cheek then took a seat at the kitchen table.

"I'm good, baby. You hungry?" she asked as she turned her fish.

"Yes, I'm starving."

"The food will be done in just a minute. I have something for you too."

"Okay. I miss you, Grandma."

"I missed you too. I was wondering why I hadn't seen you. That new position must have you busy."

"Yeah, it does. Very busy," I lied.

My grandma didn't know I killed people for a living. She thought I worked at some warehouse in Sharonville, Ohio. I couldn't let my grandma know what I did. It would kill her.

"That's good. Hard work pays off."

"Tell me about it."

My grandma set my plate of fish and fries in front of me. She made her plate then sat down to say grace. I loved my nana so much, and she reminded me so much of my mother. She was just an older version of her. They looked just alike; the only difference was my grandma was shorter than my mother. Not a day goes by that I don't think about her. If only I had pulled up two minutes earlier, I could've probably saved my mother's life.

That shit still replayed in my head like it was yesterday. The more I thought about it, the more I still wanted to kill all them motherfuckers. I swore on my soul that if I ever find out who did it, they were going to pay for it with their life.

After we finished eating, we went to look in my grandma's photo book. A tear dropped down my face when I saw my mother and father's wedding picture. I hated that our family had fallen apart because of some coward ass niggas. Me and my grandma laughed and cried at some of the pictures.

"Baby, I will be right back."

My grandma walked into the other room and came back. She had a white envelope in her hand as she sat down on the couch next to me.

"Grandson, you know I love you, and you're all I got. I appreciate everything you do for me."

"You're welcome. I told you I was going to take care of you."

"I know, and I love you for that."

"I love you too."

She handed me the envelope.

"I hope this isn't no money, Grandma, because if it is, you can have this back."

She giggled. "No, it's not money."

My phone rang and interrupted our conversation. I glanced down at the phone and it was Chief. When I answered, I and told him I would call him right back. I hadn't seen my grandmother in a while, and I wasn't about let anyone take this time away. After me and my grandma finished talking, I left. Soon as I got in the car, I called chief back.

"What's good, Chief?"

"Nothing much. How's everything going with Jada?"

"Good. Why, what's up?"

"I just wanted to make sure she was still alive."

"Why wouldn't she be? You asked me not to kill her, remember?"

"Yeah, I remember. Keep her there until I give you further instructions."

"Alright." We disconnected the call, and I glanced over at the white envelope on the passenger seat. I was anxious to open it and see what was in there.

When I pulled to up to the house, I put my car in park and grabbed the envelope off the seat then opened it. It was a letter.

Dear son,

Long time no hear. I know you probably wondering what I'm doing writing you after all these years. Truth is, I love you, and I miss you, son. When your mother passed away, that shit took a toll on me. I blamed myself for her death still to this day. I can't even explain the pain I felt when them motherfuckers took her away from me. She was my everything, and I couldn't imagine life without her. It hurts me that I had to leave you because I know you needed me, even though you were a grown man. I still wasn't there. I didn't run because I was coward, you know that. I ran because if I didn't, I would've been in jail for life or dead.

Don't get me wrong, I want revenge on all them motherfuckers who killed your mother. Back then, I couldn't really explain to you what was going on because I didn't want you involved in the bullshit. I had already lost your mother, and I wasn't about to lose my only son. Yeah, I know I fucked up, but shit, I'm human. I hope you don't hold this shit over my head.

When I left, I didn't get to tell you the story behind everything, but I think you deserve to know. I promise to tell you everything son. Just know that your mother didn't deserve what happened to her. I was set up by some coward ass niggas, if you know what mean. I should've killed them motherfuckers when I had a chance. I need to talk to you because I have some important information that I think you need to know. I'm not going to hold you up, just know I will be to see you soon, sooner than you think. Son, make sure you burn this letter because I don't need anyone to know we had contact. I will be in touch.

Love, Pops

I tore the letter into tiny pieces. When I got in the house, I flushed it down the toilet. I was happy to hear from my pops, to be honest. I had been wondering was he dead or alive since I hadn't heard from him since the day after my mother died. I wasn't mad at my pops; I had no reason to be. I knew he left for a good reason. He had to do what he had to do to protect me and himself. I didn't blame him because if I had been accused of a murder I didn't do, I would left too.

I do wish he would've written me sooner, though, but there's a reason behind everything. I walked in and Smoke was sitting in the living room watching Scarface. That's was one of his favorite movies, and that nigga swore up and down he was him. I chuckled as I made my way upstairs to check on Jada and her friend.

When I walked in, I was amazed by what I saw.

"Damn, nigga, can you knock?" Jada grabbed the towel off the floor and tried to cover her body.

I bit my bottom lip as I stared at her sexy body.

"Umm, hello? Can I have some privacy please? It's bad enough I'm locked in this damn room like a prisoner," she stated.

"Damn, my bad. Did smoke give you them clean clothes?"

"Yeah. Why you think I was taking a shower? Now get out before I put you out."

I chuckled at her little cute attitude. That shit turned me on.

"My bad. I didn't know you was naked," I said as I walked out the door.

"Niggas don't have no respect," I heard her say when I shut the door.

I walked down the hall to check on the other girl, and she was passed out. I went back downstairs, and Smoke was heading out the door.

"Where you headed?" I asked as I poured myself a well needed drink.

"To the strip club to see these hoes."

I laughed. "You coming back to the spot or you going to your house?"

"Nah, I'll be back."

"Alright."

I sat on the couch, and my phone rang. I glanced down and saw that it was Takira.

"What does she want?" I said to myself.

I pressed decline and turned my phone off. I wasn't ready to talk to Takira right now.

Smoke

The way the stripper was grinding on me had my dick hard as hell. She was a new face in the club, and she was sexy as fuck. I had fucked most of the females who danced there except for two of them, and the only reason I didn't fuck them is that they were gay. I mean, I probably could've still fucked, but I didn't even bother to try.

After I finished getting a lap dance, I had a couple of drinks and kicked it with a couple of my boys.

"Where the fuck my husband at?" Takira asked with her arms folded over her chest.

"I don't know. Why you are asking me? That's your husband."

My boys laughed.

If Takira didn't know where Killa was, I was sure it was for a damn good reason. I didn't know what was going on between them, and I damn sure wasn't about to get in the middle of it.

"I know you're lying, Smoke. G-Money, where your boy at?" she asked Killa's boy, G.

"I don't know. I haven't heard from him."

"I know yawl fucking lying."

"Bruh, don't nobody got to lie to your ass. Get the fuck out of here with that shit."

Takira sucked her teeth then gave me the middle finger. "Tell him I said when he gets a chance to call me."

She rolled her eyes and walked toward the exit.

I called Killa's phone, but it kept going to voicemail. When I tried again, it did the same thang. I chilled for a little while longer then made my way back to the safe house.

Takira

I knew Smoke was lying about where Killa was. He knew exactly where his ass was. I followed Smoke as he pulled out from the club. We drove for at least thirty minutes before he came to a stop.

"I knew that motherfucker was lying," I shouted when I saw Deron's car in the driveway.

I waited for Smoke to go in the house then parked on the opposite side of the street. Then I turned my lights off and called my girl, Princess.

"Bitch, I found Deron!"

"How?"

"I followed Smoke from the strip club to some house in Indian Hills."

"Okay, how do you know Deron is in there?"

"Because I see his car in the driveway. I'm about to knock on the door."

"Maybe they are working. I don't think it's a good idea for you to do that, Takira."

"Please, my husband is in there. I need to find out what's going on. This is my chance to find out if he is cheating on me."

"Takira, I think you're taking this too far. What if you walk in on them working? Then what? You don't know what's going on."

"Yeah, you right, but I need to know. Call you in a minute."

"Takira?" I heard Princess say before I hung up on her.

I grabbed my mace out the glove compartment and stuck it in my back pocket before I made my way to the door. When I put my ear to the door, all I heard was the television. I knocked, and minutes later, I was staring down the barrel of a gun.

"It's me, Deron, put your gun down," I stated with my hands up.

"Takira, what the fuck are you doing here?" he asked as he snatched me into the house.

"I'm looking for my husband, that's what I'm doing here. What bitch you here with?" I scanned the house with my eyes.

"How you even knew I was here?"

"Smoke told me," I lied then gave a smile.

"Ahy, yo, Smoke? Come here for a second.

Smoke came downstairs smoking a joint "What's up?"

"You told her where the fuck I was?"

"Hell nah! I told her I didn't know where you were."

"Here you go with that lying shit, Takira," Deron said.

"Whatever. I know y'all hiding something." I pushed past them and made my way upstairs.

Smoke followed me as Deron watched. I opened the first door, only to find some bitch laid up in the bed in a t-shirt.

"Oh, hell nah. Who is this bitch, Deron?" I yelled.

"Bitch, I got your bitch, hoe!" The girl got out the bed and started walking toward me, but Smoke got in the middle of us.

"Takira, chill out. This my company," Smoke admitted.

"Y'all must take me for some type of fool."

"Takira, get off that bullshit before I beat your ass," Deron said as he made his way up the stairs.

I opened the other door, and the room was empty. Then I walked down to the last door and opened it. I'll be damned if there wasn't another hoe laid up in the bed sleep.

"Un, un, Deron, who is this bitch?" Deron grab me before I could snatch that bitch off the bed.

He shut the door back and slammed me against the wall.

"How dare you bring your ass in here like you fucking running something. Don't worry about who she is."

Tears filled my eyes. "You cheating on me, Deron, are you serious?"

"Man, ain't nobody cheating on your ass! I'm here handling business. I shouldn't have to explain shit to your ass anyway. Go fuck that nigga you were with in Mexico."

I sucked my teeth. "Prove I was with another man, Deron. Where is your proof?"

"That hotel receipt was my proof."

Although Deron was right, I wasn't about to admit to the shit. I was innocent until proven guilty. What I wanted to know was who was the bitch lying in the bed sleep. I couldn't see her face because her back was turned toward the door.

"Whatever. I wasn't with nobody else. Don't try to change the subject. Who is the bitch in the room?"

"Man, get the fuck out, Takira. Bye!"

"I'm not going no fucking where. I pushed Killa away from me and opened the room door again.

"Excuse me!" I yelled at the top of my lungs. "Who the fuck is you?"

By this time, the girl was getting out the bed. When I saw it was King's girlfriend, my heart dropped.

"Oh, you know who the fuck I am!" The girl charged toward me and grabbed my hair. She hit me one good time in my face before Deron broke it up.

I ran down the stairs and out the door to my car. Nah, I didn't run because I was scared; Lord knows I would've torn her ass up. I ran because I knew it was only a matter of time before she told my husband everything, and that's if he didn't already know. How in the hell did those two know each other? Either they were fucking, or it could've been true that it was work related. Whatever it was, I wasn't taking any chances.

Killa

"Damn, shorty. What the fuck is the problem swinging on my wife like that?" I asked Jada as I stood in front of her.

"Wife?" She laughed.

"What the fuck is so funny?"

"I think you need to ask your wife," Jada stated as she took a seat on the edge of the bed.

"My wife not here, so I'm asking your ass," I said with an attitude.

"Oh, well they have this thing called a phone. How it works is you dial the person's number, and then the person will answer. After the person answers, you talk or ask them questions."

I grab Jada by the throat and pushed her back on the bed "Look, I'm not on your little sarcastic ass mouth. Either you tell me what the fuck you are talking about or I'm going blow your fucking brains out." I loosened my grip from around Jada's neck. "Now, speak."

I could see the fear in in Jada's eyes. She was so fucking cute, and I felt bad for choking her up. I hated when people played games with me, though, and I needed to know what she knew.

"Okay, I will tell you. Well, not too long ago, I decided to come home early and surprise my fiancé. I cooked dinner for him and put on my sexy lingerie."

"Get to the point. You taking too long," I stated.

"Look, you ask for the story. Shut up so you can hear it. If you're talking while I'm talking, then you can't hear me." She smiled.

I was minutes away from smacking her ass, but I decided not to. Plus, I wasn't the type of man to put my hand on a woman. I might choke or grab them up, but that's it.

"Okay, I'm listening."

"Anyway, like I was saying until I was rudely interrupted. I cooked and put on some sexy lingerie. I had the house smelling good and candles lit. Then I heard a noise. At first, I didn't know where it came from. So, I grabbed a knife and searched my house, but I didn't find anything. I heard the noise again. This time, I was sure it came from the basement. I made my way downstairs, only to see my fiancé fucking the shit out your wife."

When those words left Jada's mouth, my heart stopped then started back seconds later. I ran out the room and got in my car. Doing a hundred down the highway, I was headed to kill my wife without a doubt. Nothing could save to her ass, not even God himself. That explained why Takira ran out the house so fast. She knew Jada was going to tell me everything she knew. I knew my wife was on some bullshit, I was just praying that she wasn't.

I pulled up to my house and made my way in. I searched my house from top to bottom, and Takira was nowhere to be found. If she wasn't there, I knew she was at Princess' house. Being at Princess' house wasn't going to stop me from killing her ass.

I pulled up to princess' house, and sure enough, I saw Takira's car. I got out the car and shot every tire out to make sure my wife couldn't run anywhere. When I got to the door, I banged like I was the Cincinnati police. Seconds later, Princess opened the door.

"Where the fuck your friend at?" I asked.

"I don't know. She isn't here."

"Stop fucking lying. I see her car right there." I pushed Princess out my way and invited myself in.

I search every room except one. When I turned the doorknob, the door was locked. I kicked the door in, and Takira was standing in the corner shaking and crying.

"So, this what the fuck you do to me, bitch?" I smacked Takira so hard her mother felt it.

She fell to the floor, and I picked her up by her throat and slammed her back on the floor. "You're fucking another nigga with what belongs to me."

"Killa, stop. Please!" Princess yelled as she stood in the door with the phone in her hand.

I grabbed my gun off my waist and pointed it toward Princess "Bitch, shut up before I kill your ass."

I let off a warning shot in the air, and Princess stood there shaking like a leaf on a damn tree.

"Bitch, I gave you everything, and this how you repay me? I wrapped one of my hands around her throat and choked the shit out of her. Bitch, say your prayers." I put the gun in her mouth and cocked it back. "I love you, and your hurt me, bitch! Never again."

"Deron, no! She's pregnant!" Princess shouted as tears ran down her face.

I look over at Princess then back at Takira. She was crying and red as hell. I was at a loss for words, and I didn't know what the hell to do. At this point, I was disgusted with my wife. I didn't even want to look at her ass unless she was dead.

"Is this true, Takira?"

She nodded yes.

I removed the gun from her mouth. "Is it mine?" She nodded yes again.

Damn, I can't see myself killing my unborn child, I thought. The baby has nothing to do with it, but this bitch needed to die.

"Sir, put your hands behind your head, I heard the police say."

"Fuck!" I shouted.

The police grabbed the gun out my hand then slammed me to the floor.

"Get the fuck off me, yo."

"Ma'am, are you okay?" another officer asked.

Takira nodded. The officer handcuffed me and read me my rights. He walked me outside and threw me in back of the police car.

"Is this what you do? You beat women?" the officer asked as he pulled off.

"Man, fuck you! I bet if you didn't have that badge on, I would beat your ass too."

"Hey, watch it, buddy. You're digging a deeper hole for yourself."

I could tell this motherfucker was nothing but a prejudiced ass red neck. The whole ride to jail, all I could think about was what Princess said. I couldn't believe that Takira was pregnant. Now, the question is, who is the baby daddy? Me or the other man? I got sick to my stomach thinking about that shit.

My wife was supposed to be mine and nobody else's. No one was supposed to see her naked or see her body but me. Nobody was supposed to kiss or make love to her but me. Call me a sucker for love all you want, but Takira Marie Hutchins belonged to me. Well, at least I thought she did.

If the baby is mine, I want nothing to do with her ass after she has it. Matter of fact, Takira won't even live to see the baby that long after she has it. I promise to kill her ass and send her body to her mother. Mark my words.

We pulled up to the Hamilton County justice center, and the officers walked me to intake. They searched me, took my information, fingerprinted me, and took my picture.

"Sir, you get one free call," the lady stated.

I called Smoke to let him know what was going on.

"Who this?" Smoke answered.

"It's me. I'm locked up."

"Damn, what happened?"

"I don't have to time to explain that shit right now. I got court in the morning at 9:00 a.m. courtroom B. Tell Dame or G-money to come down here and bail me out in the morning."

"Alright, I got you. I can come if you want me to."

"Nah, I need you to stay there and watch Jada and Star."

"Alright, see you tomorrow."

"Alright." we disconnected the call."

The next morning

The bailiff came to get me for court, and I waited for them to call my name.

"Deron Hutchins."

The bailiffs open the door, so I could walk in, and I made my way to the front of the court.

"Deron Hutchins, you have been charged with domestic violence, carrying a concealed weapon, and criminal damage to personal property. How do you plead?" the judge asked.

"No contest," I replied.

"Your bond is $32,500 with 10%. Your next court date is set a month from now."

The secretary typed everything up, and my public defender handed me my paperwork. The bailiffs took me back to my cell. Hours later, I was bailed out by G-money.

"What's up, bruh? What happened?" he asked as he dapped me up.

"I will tell you when we get in the car."

We made our way to the car, and I got in.

"That bitch Takira been cheating on me."

G looked at me like I was crazy. "What? That's some bullshit. I saw her ass in the club like a week ago."

"Damn, for real?" I shook my head. I had asked Takira to stay out the club, and she still was sneaking behind my back. "I'm done with that bitch. I want a divorce.

"I'm surprised her ass is still alive," G Money stated.

"If Princess would've never said Takira was pregnant, and the police didn't bust through the door, she would've been as good as dead."

G shook his head because he felt my pain. Years ago, he caught his wife cheating. The only difference is, he killed her, and nobody ever found her body. Everybody thought she ran off with the other man. Little did they know that both of them were dead.

"I don't blame you. That's some disrespectful bullshit. When you're married, your wife belongs to you and nobody else. Whoever that nigga is, he got to get his issue too."

"You already know when I find out who it is, it's on, G."

"You know you don't even have to do nothing. I got you, my nigga."

"Yeah, I know you do, but I want that nigga all to myself."

G drove me back to Princess' house so I could get my car. Once he saw that I was in the car, we both pulled off. I got a text from Chief saying he need to see me in his office as soon as possible, so I headed to his place of business. Before I got out the car, I called

Smoke to make sure the girls were okay. He informed me that everything was okay.

I got out and walked into the building that Chief had in Loveland. Chief had bought a big office park building in Loveland, Ohio. Each office was filled with workers. One office might be bagging Kush while the people in the other office were making meth. Each office had some type of supplies in it with workers. There was even an office there that workers could go in to fuck a prostitute. The building was secured, and cameras were everywhere. Chief even had two Loveland police officers guarding the doors. They were crooked ass cops, and they didn't care what Chief did. Chief was paying them more than the city of Loveland was anyway.

I got on the elevator and pressed five. The elevator dinged and I was on the fifth floor. I knocked on the door, and Chief invited me in.

"Take a seat," he said as soon as I came through the door.

I glanced at the dude who was sitting in the other seat. I really didn't pay attention to him, though, because I don't like niggas at all.

"I want you to meet somebody."

I didn't know what the fuck Chief was on, but he already knew I didn't fuck with people I didn't know.

"I'm good," I said to Chief.

"Look, I know you don't fuck with people, Killa, but he's part of the team. I mean, everybody on the team respects and looks up to you, and I want you to meet him because, for one, he's my son, and for two, he about to be running the business soon. I decided to move out of town and run the other office I have in Cali."

"Look, I don't need to meet nobody. If you are moving, cool. I'm not about to work for no other motherfucker unless it's myself. No disrespect to your son, but I'm cool," I said as I sat at the edge of my chair.

"I understand that, but I need you on my team."

"No disrespect, Pops, but I don't need that nigga. I got hittas on my team," his son blurted out.

When those words came out his mouth, I stood to my feet. In my eyes, that was a fucking threat.

"What the fuck that mean?" I asked as I stared at his ass.

"Exactly what the fuck I said," he replied as he stood to his feet.

"Out of respect for your father, I'm not going to beat your ass then murder you. I don't want him to have to bury his son because he is talking shit." I laughed.

"Ahy, both of y'all stop!" Chief blew smoke from his cigar.

"Look, Killa, I look at you as a son, and I would never disrespect you. I just want you to stay on the team for me. I know your skills are good, and my son would be good if he needs you. I will triple your pay."

Now Chief was talking. When he said triple, he caught my attention. I was all about money and willing to do anything to stop this lifestyle. Tripling my money would definitely help me retire from this shit sooner than I thought.

"Man, I told you, Pops. I'm good on this weak ass nigga."

"Weak as nigga?"

Before I knew it, I hit his son in the jaw, and he fell to the ground.

Chief put his cigar out in the ashtray and stood in front me. Even though Chief had clout, he knew not to cross me, especially over his son. I would shoot both of their ass and be running his business.

"Was that necessary, Killa?" Chief asked.

"Hell yeah, it was. Ain't shit weak about me, nigga. Tell your son to respect his elders." I stood there and waited for him to get up so I could knock his ass out again.

Chief walked over to his son and helped him off the floor. "King, get up and apologize to Killa."

"Man, I'm not apologizing to him."

"You heard what I said. Do it now, or you won't have a position in my empire."

"My bad, bruh," King said and then walked out the door and slammed it behind him.

I could tell that his son was a straight pussy. There was no way in hell I would apologize to a grown ass man. I would've just had to take that loss. If I wasn't mistaken, that was the same dude, I saw at the restaurant that day in the car. He was the quiet one; I guess he knew I would kill his ass. I talked to Chief for a little while longer, and he told me he would hit me up soon about Jada. He was waiting for an important call. I told him okay and to just let me know.

After that, I made my way back to Indian Hills where we were keeping the girls. When I walked in, I didn't see Smoke anywhere in sight.

"Smoke?" I called out, but he didn't answer.

I figured his ass was in the shower. He was definitely there because his Benz was parked outside.

I made my way upstairs to check on the girls. I walked into the room where Star was being held, and all I could do was laugh on the inside. Star was riding the fuck out of Smoke. I shook my head and eased the door shut. Star was pretty, but she didn't have shit on Jada.

Jada was sexy as hell with long, black, silky hair that hung down her back. She was light skinned and thick. Her small waist complemented her frame. Not to mention her round ass. Star had milk chocolate skin with pretty white teeth. She stood about 5'7" and she was slim built but proportioned just right.

I walked down to Jada's room and used my key to get in. She was sitting up in the bed.

"What you want?" she said soon as I walked in the door.

"You still haven't learned your lesson, huh?"

"What lesson? Oh, you a teacher now?"

I laughed because her little smart-ass mouth turned me on. "Nah, I'm not a teacher, but I can teach you something. For instance, I can teach you how to talk to adults with respect."

She rolled her eyes. "Is that what you call yourself?" She laughed.

"You hungry?" I asked, ignoring her sarcastic comment.

"Yeah, actually I am. Can you get me some Chipotle with extra white rice, corn, extra chicken, extra cheese, and some sour cream, please?"

I chuckled as I leaned against the wall. "You think I'm about to get you some Chipotle with that smart-ass mouth?" I laughed. "You can get a peanut butter and jelly, a bologna sandwich, or some chicken or beef ramen noodles. Choose wisely, I don't have all day."

I smiled because I knew I had pissed her off.

Jada sucked her teeth. "Don't nobody want y'all jail meals. I would rather starve. Just bring me a cup of water."

"Hot or cold?"

"Hot, so I can toss it in your damn face."

I shook my head and laughed then walked out the room. When I walked out, Smoke was coming out the room with a big ass smile on his face.

"Nigga, what you so happy about?" I asked as if I didn't know.

"Man, shorty pussy is good as fuck. I just piped her ass down good. Bruh, I think I'm in love."

I laughed hysterically because I knew Smoke didn't just say what I think he said. This was the same person who told me he would never fall in love with no woman.

"You in love, Smoke? Get the fuck out of here."

"I'm for real, and she's crazy as me."

"What makes you say that?"

"When you were locked up, we had a big ass argument, and she swung on me. You know me, I slapped the shit out her ass. That bitch squared up with me like she was a nigga. She swung on me and hit me with some shit. I can't lie, my dick instantly got hard."

I burst out laughing. "Hold that thought. I gotta hit up Uber Eats and ordered Chipotle for Jada and her friend." I didn't know what her friend liked but I was sure they liked the same thing.

Even though I told her I wasn't going to buy her shit, I lied. I was just making her ass suffer because of her smart-ass mouth.

While we waited, Smoke told me about how everything went down with him and Star. When he was done, I told him why I was locked up. He was shocked to know that Takira had cheated on me and even more surprised that she was alive and not dead yet. Bad as I wanted to kill her, I couldn't until I found out if the baby was mine.

I always wanted a family, but sorry to say it won't be with Takira's ass. It was fucked up because I always thought she would be the one to have all my kids. I never pictured life without Takira. I loved that girl to death and would give her anything she wanted. Too bad she didn't feel the same way about me. Every time I thought about Takira, I wanted to go snap her neck. I hated that bitch with every fiber in my body.

The Uber Eats driver knocked on the door, and I got the food then handed Smoke Star's food. I took it upstairs to Jada.

"What you want? Why you keep coming in here?" Jada rolled her neck.

I walked over to her and set the food in front of her. "You're welcome."

She sucked her teeth. "Whatever."

"What's up with you and that smart mouth?"

She grabbed her food out the bag like she didn't hear me talking to her.

"Your deaf now?" I asked.

"Oh, my bad, I didn't hear you. What you say?" she asked sarcastically.

I said what's up with you and that smart-ass mouth."

"I didn't realize my mouth was smart."

I leaned over in Jada's face. "I would let you have it, but you're so cute, my heart won't allow it."

A smiled crept across her face then quickly disappeared. "Anyway…"

"Yeah, I know. Anyway," I stated right before I left the room.

I went back downstairs so Smoke could finish telling me the story about him and Star.

Takira

I hated that me and Deron were on bad terms. I loved and missed him so much, and I had been calling him all day, but he hadn't been answering my calls. I knew he was mad at me, but all I wanted to do was fix our marriage. Any chance I had with my husband was blown when I showed up at that house. There was no way in hell he would get back with me after what happened. I was lucky to even be alive to tell my story.

I can't lie, I was kind of mad at Princess for telling Deron I was pregnant. I had just found out a couple days ago, but I wasn't planning to tell Deron because I was going to have an abortion. The baby could be Deron's or King's, and I didn't want to take any chances. Now that

Princess had let the cat out the bag, I had to go with the flow. I was mad at Princess, but I knew she only did it to save my life.

When Deron went to jail, my feelings were hurt. I was going to bail him out, but I was terrified to see him. I had never seen my husband that mad. The rage in his eyes let me know he wanted my blood. I was scared as shit and just knew my life was over. I can't tell you how many times I prayed within those minutes. God had to have been tired of hearing me.

I wanted to call King and tell him that Jada was fucking Killa. The only reason I didn't call was that it was already enough drama going on, and I didn't know if they were actually fucking. Plus, King already hated my husband for whatever reason. Me telling King right now wasn't going to bring my husband back.

I only had nine months to convince my husband not to kill me. Once I had this baby, if I have it, I would be good as dead. I rode over to my house to see if Killa was home, but his car wasn't there. I went in the house to see had he been there. Everything was still the same way he left it.

I picked our wedding picture up off the nightstand and tears filled the rim of my eyes right before they fell down my cheeks. I had the best man in the world, and I messed up. There was no way I would give up that easily, though. I loved Deron, and I was going to do whatever it took to prove to him that I'm sorry.

After I grabbed a couple of my belongings, I made my way out the door. I sat in the car for a while crying my eyes out. All I wanted to do was come home and be a family again.

Jada

Thoughts of King crossed my mind as I lay in bed. I couldn't believe what he had done to me. I was months away from marrying the man of my dreams, and I thought King would never cheat on me again. Thought he really loved me, but I guess not. I had turned down all types of men for King, and he couldn't turn down one woman for me? There was no telling how many other women he had slept with or had in our home. The thought made me want to vomit. I wanted nothing more that to kill King for the pain he caused me.

I had even gone against my father for this man, and this was the thanks I got. I hadn't talked to my father in months, all because he told me that King wasn't the one.

My father told me he didn't trust King, and it was something about him. My father was a street nigga back in the day. He told me it was two kinds of street niggas; the real ones and the fake ones. The real ones are the ones hustling to make ends meet and stacking to get a better life. The fake ones are out here doing anything just to say they did it and didn't know shit about the streets.

My father said he felt like King was a fake, disloyal ass bitch. Sad to say, my father was right. King was everything my father said he was. I wished I could hug my father and just tell him he was right. I miss my dad so much, and I hated that I didn't listen. Like my mother used to say, a hard head makes a soft ass. I was paying for it with tears and pain. I had never felt so hurt and humiliated in my life.

I wipe the tears from my eyes and stared at the ceiling.

"You alright?" Killa asked as he stood in the doorway.

"Do I look okay? I've been kidnapped, and I don't know why?"

"Shit, me either. I'm just doing my job."

"Is that what you call it?" I rolled my eyes and sat up in the bed. "I'm tired of being here, and I'm ready to go. I do have a life outside these walls."

Killa shut the door behind him "Shit, I do too. You think I like babysitting? I'm not no damn nanny."

"Well, you good at it, so you should be one."

Killa laughed out loud and walked over to the bed. "You need a hug?"

"No, not from you."

"I'm going to give you one anyway."

Killa reached down and hugged me. I tried to push him off me, but he had a tight hold. Honestly, it felt good to be in a man's arms. I should've been given him a hug because I knew he was hurt after what I told him about his wife. I was hurt, and King wasn't even my husband. I could only imagine how Killa felt being married.

I broke down on Killa's shoulder. "Why he hurt me like this?" I cried.

Killa comforted me as I soaked his shirt with my tears. "He doesn't deserve you and you don't deserve him. any man who can't see what he got in front of him is blind."

"I did everything for him, and he promised he wouldn't hurt me no more," I sobbed.

"If that nigga hurts you, he never loved you. Love isn't supposed to hurt. I don't care what y'all going through, a man should always keep his woman happy. What he won't do, a real man will."

I lifted my head off Killa's chest and stared deep into his eyes. Killa wiped the tears from my eyes, and before I knew it, my lips met Killa's. Our tongues wrestled, and I could feel my pussy getting moist.

Killa push me back.

"What are you doing?" I asked.

"I don't think you ready for this. Plus, you're vulnerable right now. I don't want you to make any moves that you're going to regret in the long run. Plus,

I'm not the type of man who likes to have his feelings played with."

I sucked my teeth. Maybe Killa was right. Maybe I was vulnerable at the moment, but it felt so right. Maybe I was trying to move on fast so I could get over King. I didn't know what it was, but it felt good to kiss Killa's soft lips.

"Okay, if you say so," I said with an attitude.

Killa

Damn, that kiss that me and Jada just shared had a nigga ready to make love to her. That wasn't just ol' kiss. I didn't want to stop Jada, but we both had a lot going on right now. I wasn't trying to get Jada involved in anything that was going on between me and Takira. I already knew how hot tempered Takira could be, and I wasn't trying to put Jada in that predicament. Not saying that Jada couldn't handle her own, but I didn't like drama, especially not between two females.

I had to figure out what I was going to do about Takira anyway. A part of me wanted to give it another chance for the sake of my baby, but I couldn't. Once you cross me, you will do that shit again, and I don't trust it.

I hated the fact that my wife was pregnant with my supposed to be baby, and we wouldn't be raising him or her together.

I had always told Takira that I wanted a family. I wanted a big ass family for real with many little ones running around. Too bad I was going to be raising this baby myself because I doubt if I let Takira live. I knew I said I was going to kill her; I had just been second guessing myself. I didn't want my child to not have a mother like I did. That shit hurt like hell, and it still hurts till this day. I didn't want my child to go through that growing up. I knew the questions would come when my child got older. He or she would want to know what happened to their mother, and I wouldn't be able to tell him or her that I killed her because she was a worthless hoe.

I still wanted Takira dead, but I just had to make the right decision for my child *if* it's my child. I did know one thing, though. I didn't want to be with Takira. There was nothing she could say or do to make me change my mind. The thought of another man touching what belonged to me had me livid.

When I find out who he is, I was still going to kill his ass. I wanted to ask Jada his name, but I knew she had a lot on her mind. Plus, if he came up missing, I didn't want her to know I killed his ass. Jada still had love for him, and I didn't need her telling the cops shit if I did take him out. She would slip and say who he was sooner or later, though, and that's when the beast in me would demolish his ass.

I told smoke I would be back and that I had to handle some business. After I went downtown to see my lawyer, I went to check on my house. I called Takira and told her to meet me at the house because I needed to talk to her as soon as possible. I waited in the living room, and Takira pulled up minutes later.

Soon as she walked in, she ran over and gave me a hug. I didn't hug her back. Instead, I pushed her off me.

"Baby, please stop acting like this. I miss you so much, Deron." She began to cry.

"Nah, you miss that nigga you were fucking."

"Deron, I'm sorry." She cried even harder."

"How long was you fucking that nigga, huh?"

"Deron, please don't make me answer that. Please."

"You better answer it," I stated as I stood to my feet. "All the shit I did for you, Kira, and this how you repay me, huh?" I pointed my finger in her face "How long you were fucking that nigga?"

"Some months, Deron. I'm sorry." She tried to grab me, but I pushed her away like she was diseased.

"Is that my baby?"

"Yes, I swear it is."

"It better be because that's the only thing that's going to save your life, bitch. Let me find out differently, and you good as dead."

Takira backed up a couple of steps.

"Baby, can we please make this right? I promise it won't happen again."

I laughed because she must be crazy. "You think I'm going to take you back after you let another man touch what was mine? I don't eat off another man's plate. You got me fucked up. There will never be you and me again, Takira. I'm done with you. Matter of fact," I grabbed the envelope off the living room table, "here, make sure you fill that out as soon as you can."

"What's this?" Takira asked as she opened the envelope. "Really? Are you fucking serious right now, Deron?"

"Serious as a bitch that cheats," I said and grinned.

"I'm not signing shit!" Takira tore the divorce papers up and threw them on the on the floor.

I made my way to the door so I could leave.

"Please, Deron, don't leave. Baby, please," she cried as she held on to the back of my shirt. "I'm begging you.

"Get off me! I'm cool on you. You had one simple job, and that was to be a fucking wife. Instead, you want to be a hoe. You made your bed, now lie in it or die in it, Takira."

"Can we just talk about it? Please, baby. I'm begging you. I promise on my life it won't happen again." Tears ran down her pretty face, but it still wasn't enough to get me back. "Have your shit out my house by this weekend," I said and walked out the door to my car.

Takira was still calling my name and begging me not to go. She was in the doorway on her knees crying her heart out. A part of me felt bad but fuck it. She didn't care how I would feel when she fucked that nigga. The hurtful part is, the baby might not be mine. I didn't care how much Takira told me the baby was mine. I didn't believe it. I had to get a DNA test first. Takira had proven to me that she couldn't be trusted, so I damn sure couldn't take her word.

I knew one thing, she'd better have all her shit out my house soon, or I would have it remove myself. I didn't want anything that reminded me of her ass. I prayed that if the baby was mine, it didn't look shit like her.

My phone rang, interrupting my thoughts. I was about to decline it until I saw that it was Chief. I answered the phone, and he told me that he wanted me to bring Jada to the warehouse on the hills in two or three days at noon. I told him we would be there.

I didn't know what the hell Chief was on, but I knew it wasn't good. The only time we went to the hills was to kill or torture somebody. I was shocked when Chief told me to kidnap Jada and not kill her. Anybody that Chief wanted me to go after, they never lived. For some reason, he didn't want Jada to die, and I had no idea why. I guess I would find out in the next couple of days.

Jada

That kiss I shared earlier with Killa was still on my mind. My pussy was still wet, and I couldn't get him off my mind. I caressed both of my breasts and played with my hard nipples. I lifted my right breast toward my mouth and licked it. Next, I stuck my index finger and middle finger in mouth until they were completely wet. I spread my legs widely and place my finger on my clitoris then rubbed my clit in a circular motion as I closed my eyes and thought about Killa.

"Umm, shit." I let out a moan.

I then slid my index and middle finger inside me. My pussy was wet, and I couldn't wait to release my juices. I threw the cover off me because it was getting in my way. Then I caressed my right breast while I fingered my pussy fast then slow. I remove my fingers from my pussy and tasted it before I slid my fingers back in. I fingered myself fast while wishing it was Killa. I then played with my clitoris again, and I could feel my nut building up.

"Ooh shit. Uh, uh." I moaned as I came all over the sheets.

I was breathing hard like I had just got my brains fucked out. When I opened my eyes to pull up my panties, Killa was standing right there.

"Oh my God! Killa, how long you been right there?" I asked and pulled the cover over me.

"Why you stop?" he asked as he bit his bottom lip.

"I-I don't know," I stuttered. "I mean, I was done."

Killa pulled me off the bed and held me close to him. He then kissed me, and I returned the favor. My pussy was getting even wetter. Killa's 6'2" frame towered over my short body. Killa pick me up and put me against the wall. Next, he wrapped my legs around his waist and my arms around his neck. He then slowly slid his long, thick pole inside of me. Killa moved in and out of me as he kissed my neck. I moved up and down on his dick like it belonged to me.

"Damn, you gon' handle that dick like that?" Killa asked as he licked his lips.

He walked me over to the bed and lay me down then kissed my lips before he made his way down to my 36C breasts. Killa sucked on my nipple while he caressed my other breast. When he was done, he kissed down my stomach, bypassing my pussy, and down to my feet. He kissed his way back up and our lips met again. We started kissing again, and I felt Killa's dick grow harder.

"You sure you ready for this?" I questioned.

"I'm sure, Killa."

He took both of my legs and pushed them behind my head then dove balls deep into my pussy. Killa was beating the pussy like it stole something, and I couldn't take it. I pushed Killa's chest, trying to get him off me.

"Nah, take that dick, Jada," he demanded as he pinned my hands behind my head.

Killa pumped in and out of me fast.

"Aww, fuck. I feel it in my stomach," I yelled.

"That's where you supposed to feel it."

I put my legs down because I couldn't take it anymore. Killa smiled at me and turned me over on all fours.

"Damn, you sexy," he stated as he rubbed my round ass.

Killa then grabbed my tiny waist and glided every inch he had to offer inside me. I could feel him deep in me, and I could barely take it. Killa was way bigger than King, and he definitely was way rougher. I can't lie; it felt so good, but it hurt so bad.

"Ooh, fuck me harder, Killa." I moaned.

I didn't know what I was thinking when I said that because I could barely take it. My pussy was sore as hell, but I wanted that ache. I wanted to feel all of him inside me.

Killa started to pound my pussy harder without a care in the world. At this point, the pain had turned into pure pleasure. Even though my pussy was sore, I was still begging for more.

"Damn, that pussy so wet." Killa groaned as he kissed up and down my back.

I threw my ass back on him, making it jiggle. Killa release his hands off my waist as he watched me work that dick. I was a little used to the feeling by now.

"Work that dick," he stated as he smacked my ass.

I moved back and forth on that dick and made my ass cheeks move one by one. I then made my ass shake fast on his log as I slid back and forth on it.

"Aww, fuck, Jada!" He moaned.

Killa flipped me over one my back then kissed me passionately. Next, he put his log deep inside me and continued to please me.

"I want you, Jada," he said as he pushed in and out of me.

"I want you too, Killa," I replied as I fucked him back."

"Shit, I'm about to bust." Killa groaned as he bit his bottom lip.

He began to go faster and faster. Next thing I knew, he was nutting all over my stomach. Killa collapsed on top of me, and we were both breathing heavily. He rolled over on his back and lay there for a couple of minutes.

"Come on."

He grabbed my hand and walked me into the bathroom, and we took a long shower. After we were done, we talked for a while and watched a movie. I had to say, I was feeling Killa, and I wanted more than just a fuck thang. I knew it was too early to be talking about a relationship, but it was something about this man. I never knew how love at first sight felt, but I was sure it felt like this.

Takira

After Deron left, I cried a river. I didn't want him to go. I wanted to call him, but I knew it would be a waste of time. He wasn't going to answer for me. I knew one thing, though, I wasn't giving up no matter what. I was going to do whatever it took to get my husband back. I'd be damned if another woman got what belonged to me.

I lay on the couch still crying like a kid who lost her puppy. My phone rang, and I saw that it was Princess. I lay the phone down beside me because I didn't want to talk anyone if it wasn't Deron. Princess called a couple more times then sent me a text.

Princess: *Let me know you're okay, Takira, or I'm calling the police.*

Me: *Yes, I'm good. I'm at the house. He gone. He wants a divorce.*

Princess: *What? Are you serious?*

I didn't reply. All I wanted to do was lie there. I was stressing heavily, and I didn't know what to do. I didn't know how I was about to live without Deron. If it wasn't for him, I wouldn't have half the shit I had now, and I was about to lose everything including my husband. Deron was the only man I ever loved besides Tae.

Tae was my first, and I was with him for years. If he had never gotten locked up, we probably would've been married. Even after Tae got locked up, we did keep in touch until I started dating Deron, and he wasn't going for any of that. He made it clear that as long as I was his woman, I couldn't talk to other man, including Tae. I knew Deron meant what he said, so I cut Tae off.

Tae was pissed that I stopped writing him. He was even more pissed when he found out I got married. The only reason I know is because he told Princess. Tae also told her that he was going to fuck me up when he got out. Tae was crazy, but I wasn't worried about him. He knew that Deron would beat his ass and murder him. Everybody and they mama knew not to mess with Deron or his family.

After I finished lying around, I went upstairs to take a shower. Deron wanted me to have all my stuff out, but I wasn't going anywhere. I was going to fight for my husband like a wife should.

When I was done showering my phone rang. I ran over to it, praying it Deron, but it wasn't. It was King. I hadn't talked to King in some days now. He was the reason I was in this predicament now. I let my phone ring while I put on my pajamas. Then I lay across the bed and start crying again when I saw our wedding picture on the nightstand next to our bed. I hated to know that Deron didn't want me anymore. I wondered if he still loved me or thought about me sometimes.

I knew I had fucked up, but the least he could do was hear me out. I cried for the rest of the night until fell asleep.

Smoke

"I don't know why you want a DNA all of the sudden. You have never questioned if Lil Chaz was yours before," Laquisha said as we stood in front of the DNA place.

"Man, shut up."

"You shut up! Make me shut up. I'ma keep talking as long as I want to because I'm that bitch," Laquisha stated with my son on her hip.

"That's why don't I want to mess with your ratchet ass now. You do too much childish shit. Give me my son." I snatched Lil Chaz from her hands.

"Your son? You sure about that?"

"You lucky I got my son in my hands, or I would smack the shit out your ass."

"You're not going to smack shit, lame ass nigga. I will beat your ass and whoever else ass."

I walked inside the building, ignoring Laquisha's dumb ass. She trailed behind me, still talking shit and causing a scene.

"What the fuck are you looking at?" Laquisha asked some girl who was staring at her ignorant ass.

The girl rolled her eyes and didn't respond.

"Yeah, that's what I thought," Laquisha stated.

"Chill your stupid ass out, Quisha."

"Make me, make me," she said being petty.

I couldn't wait for them to call my name because I was two seconds from slapping the shit out of her. Ten minutes later, the lady called me to the back, and I took Lil Chaz with me.

"Hello, how are you?'

"I'm fine, how about you?"

"I'm blessed," the nurse said. "Hey, handsome man." She grabbed Lil Chaz's hand, and he smiled.

"Okay, I need you to open your mouth real wide for me so I can swab you," the nurse said.

I opened my mouth, and she swabbed both of my cheeks. She then put the swab into a plastic container with my name on it.

"Is this the baby getting tested?" she asked.

"Yes."

"Is the mother here? I need her permission to swab him."

"Yes, she out there. She's the loud, ratchet one."

She laughed and walked out to the lobby to ask and then came back in to swab Lil Chaz's mouth. When she was done, we walked out then she called Laquisha back. Me and Lil Chaz waited for her to come out. In the process of waiting, my phone rang. I glanced down at the phone, and it was Killa.

"What's up with it, bruh."

"Nothing much. Where your ass at? Getting some money?"

"Hell nah, I'm at the DNA place getting a test. I took your advice."

"That's what's up. I got somebody who wants to talk to you."

"Hey." A smile crept across my face when I heard Star's voice. I didn't know how the hell she gamed Killa to call me.

"What's up, baby?"

"Nothing, I miss you."

I smiled. It was something about Star that made a nigga feel good on the inside. "I miss you too."

"You miss who?" I heard Laquisha say.

"Man, gone with that bullshit, Quisha, damn."

"I will beat that bitch ass and yours," she said as she followed me out the door.

"Baby, I will see you when I get there," I told Star.

"Okay." I hung up the phone and put it in my pocket, and then I open the car door and put Lil Chaz in his car seat.

"So, that's the reason I haven't seen you? You got another bitch?" she asked, getting in my face.

"Man, watch your mouth. And if I did?"

"Oh, so you taking up for these hoes now?"

"Get the fuck out my face before I beat your ass, Quisha. I'm done with your ass. Don't call me unless it's about my son," I stated as I walked toward my car.

"Fuck you! You dumb motherfucker."

"You wish you could fuck me. I know you better not be driving crazy while my son in the car."

Laquisha got in her car and pulled off. I watched her until I couldn't see her no more because I'd be damned if she hurt my son. I was still trying to figure out how the hell did Star manage to get Killa to call me. She had to do a whole lot of begging and pleading. For the last couple of days, I had been in and out of the safe house. Chief had me delivering packages all week. I wasn't tripping, though, because I needed the money anyway.

When it comes to money, I'm all about it. Over the last couple of weeks, me and Star had gotten close. It was something about her that had me attached to her. I liked the fact that her crazy complemented mine. Even though Laquisha was crazy, I would never wife her ass. I only dealt with her because she had my son and good head.

Star was sexy, and I could tell she was on her shit from the conversations we had. I knew she wasn't no dumb ass woman. I couldn't wait to see Star because I hadn't really kicked it with her like that in the last couple of days.

When I walked in Star, Jada, and Killa were sitting in the living room. I was shocked to see that he let them both out the room.

"Killa, let me holla at you," I said as I walked into the kitchen.

What's up?"

"Why they out the room? What's gotten into your ass?"

He laughed. "They just chilling."

"You fucked didn't you?" I asked with grin on my face.

The only way I could see Killa letting Jada out was if he fucked her or he was feeling her. Even though Killa be on the mess, he did have a soft spot for women, especially after what happened to his mother.

"I don't know what you're talking about."

I laughed because I knew Killa's ass was lying like a motherfucker. This nigga was always trying to be private about what he did.

"You a motherfucker." I chuckled.

"Chief hit me up and told me he wants you to bring Jada to him in a couple of days. He doesn't even know about her friend, Star, being here. Did you tell him?"

"Nah, he wouldn't care anyway. His focus is on Jada."

"So, it's cool if we let Star go?"

"No, I don't think that's a good idea just yet. What if she calls the police because we still has Jada?"

"I don't think she will. Shorty cool as hell."

"She might be cool, but keep in mind, we don't know her. This is her best friend we are talking about, and from what Jada said, they're more like sisters."

I peeked around the corner to make sure they weren't listening. They were sitting on the couch watching television and talking.

"You right. I feel you. We can just keep her around until we find out what's going on. What we going to do about her when we go to take Jada to Chief?" I asked.

"We can either leave her here or in the van. I don't know. We will figure that shit out."

"Alright."

"What happened at the DNA place?"

I shook head and told Killa everything that went down with Laquisha's ghetto ass.

Jada

"Oh my God, you really fucked him, Star?" I asked.

"Hell yeah. It was good too."

We both laughed.

"Tell me how it all started."

"You nosey, but okay. I had just finished smoking and taking a shower. I had found half a joint in my pocket. You know me, I like to walk around naked or with my bra and panties on after showering. This night, I was lying in the bed butt ass naked and watching some *Martin* episodes. Smoke had come in to check on me, and I snapped on him. My mind was already a wreck from being kidnapped.

"Why are you in here?" I rolled my eyes.

"I'm just making sure you didn't go nowhere." He chuckled.

"I don't find shit funny."

I got up butt ass naked and walked over to him. "Get the fuck out before I beat your ass."

Smoke laughed. "That will be the day I knock a bitch out."

"Bitch, who are you calling a bitch?"

"The bitch who asking is who I'm calling a bitch."

I punched him in his chest, and he picked me up then slammed me down on the bed. Smoke got on top of me and pinned my hands behind my head.

"I will fuck your sexy ass up."

Smoke looked into my eyes, and at that moment, I felt something.

"What? You felt something? What you feel? His dick growing through his pants? Because I know it wasn't love," I stated, interrupting her story.

We both burst out laughing.

"I felt something special."

"Umm hmm. Continue."

"Anyway, back to what I was saying before I was rudely interrupted." We both chuckled.

"Next thing I know, Smoke's lips were pressed against mine. He kissed me, and I kissed him. He released my arms and kissed all over my body. Then he made it to my kitty and kissed all over it. When I felt his tongue separate my pussy lips, and he took my clit into his mouth, my body completely shut down. He was licking and slurping all on my pussy. I grabbed his head and moved up and down on his face. I came at least twice before he slid it in."

"Y'all did use a condom, right?"

"No. Stop interrupting me, please and thank you. Hold all your questions till the end damn."

"After he beat the pussy from the back, he roughly flipped me over and placed my legs on his shoulders. I told him to let me ride him, and he wasted no time lying down. I placed my hands on my knees and started bouncing up and down. I was riding the shit out of him and enjoying every minute of it. Next thing I know, Smoke said he was about to nut. The dick was so good, I couldn't get up, and Smoke nutted all in me. After that, we smoked a Kush joint."

I covered my mouth. "Oh my God, are you serious? What if you get pregnant?"

"Girl, I don't care. With dick like that, he can get me pregnant whenever. Not to mention that good ass tongue."

We both chuckled.

"You a hot mess, Star."

"So, what's up with you and Killa?"

"Nothing," I quickly answered. "What are you talking about?"

Star crossed her arms over her chest and twisted her lips "You must think I'm stupid, don't you? I didn't meet you yesterday at a PTA meeting, Jada"

"What? Nothing happened," I said, trying not to look at Star. I knew if anyone knew when I was lying, it was her.

"Oh my God. You fucked him, didn't you?"

"Shh! Can you keep your voice down?" I said.

Star started jumping up and down and holding her chest like she was dying "You got to tell me what happened, girl. I knew he was going to get your ass, I knew it. I don't know about you, but I love being kidnapped," Star stated with a big smile on her face.

"Will you calm down?" I grabbed Star's arm and pulled her back down on the couch.

"Shh, be quiet before they hear you."

"Girl, you got to tell me what the fuck happened." Star was happier that I got some dick than me.

"Okay, I will tell you. Just be quiet."

Star sat back on the couch with a big smile on her face "Okay, I'm waiting. My best friend got some dick. My best friend got some dick," Star said, making a song out of it.

All I could do was laugh at her ignorant ass. Before I could tell her what happened, Killa and Smoke came out the kitchen.

"What's so funny?" Killa asked as he glanced at me and Star.

"Right. We want to laugh too." Smoke added his two cents.

"Nothing. We was just laughing at what was on TV," Star replied.

Killa looked back at the television, only to see the news on. "What's funny about the news? The part where he talks about the weather or the part where he talks about who died today?"

Smoke laughed at Killa's smart ass remark.

Star sucked her teeth. "You got a smart-ass mouth just like my friend, Jada. I like you. Maybe y'all should hook up."

Killa cracked a smile. "Maybe we should."

"This isn't Love Connection. Don't be trying to hook my boy up with nobody. He a grown ass man, and he doesn't need your help," Smoke stated.

"Smoke, shut the fuck up. Before I smack your ass," Star responded.

"Nah, you shut up before I smack that ass," Smoke said as he rubbed Star's ass.

Star laughed. "Stop. You play too much, Smoke."

"I'm trying to play with something else."

"That's all you had to say?" Star got off the couch and walked toward the room.

"I will be in there soon as I finish rolling this joint," Smoke stated.

Killa laughed "You crazy, man. Y'all two meant for each other, and I don't even know her. I can honestly say that I like her better than Laquisha.

"Laquisha? Who is Laquisha?" I asked with an attitude.

"Smoke's baby mama. Why? You questioning this man like he yours. What's up with that?"

"Killa, whatever. Don't start with me because I'm not the one."

"What's that supposed to mean, Jada? I told you about that sassy ass mouth."

My sassy ass mouth? You just got smart with me. I asked Smoke a simple question, and you jumped your ass in the conversation.

Smoke laughed and started shaking his head. "You telling me y'all haven't fucked." Smoke chuckled "That's a damn lie." Smoke lit his joint and stood to his feet "I'm going to let y'all two lovebirds argue. I will be back after I put your friend to sleep.

I looked over at Killa and rolled my eyes.

"Don't get them eyes knocked on the floor," Killa jokingly said.

"Whatever," I replied and waved him off.

Killa sat next to me and kissed me on the cheeks.

"Move. I don't know where your lips been."

"I'm trying to put them on you."

I giggled. Killa's phone started to ring, ruining the moment. I looked out the corner of my eye to see who was calling. When I saw he had his wife saved under *This Cheating Ass Bitch,* I almost burst out laughing. He declined the call and set the phone down on his lap. I moved the phone and climbed on top of him. Killa wrapped his arms around my waist and kissed me on my neck.

"You better stop before you start something, Jada."

"Whatever I start, baby, trust me I can finish."

Killa bit his bottom lip then smacked my ass. His phone started to ring again, and we looked down at it at the same time. I pushed the phone to the side and kissed him again. I could feel his manhood rising through his pants. My pussy got wet, and I couldn't wait to feel him inside me.

I grind on his dick, making it even harder. Killa pulled my tights over my ass. I stood up so I could pull my tights all the way down, and Killa took his pants and boxers off. I sat back on top of him and glided down on his long penis.

"Umm, shit." I moaned as I worked my pussy muscles to adjust to his dick.

When it was finally in, I moved up and down on his manhood. Killa laid his head back on the couch and closed his eyes. He was so into it that he didn't even realize his phone was ringing. I pressed the answer button and gave his wife a taste of her own medicine.

"That pussy feels so good, baby." Killa groaned.

"How good it feel, daddy?"

"Real good."

I don't know what was turning me on more. The fact that he was talking to me or the fact that I knew his wife was listening. I bounce up and down on his dick, and I could feel my pussy splashing all over him.

"Damn, you wet as fuck. Ride that shit, baby." Killa smacked my ass, causing me to go wild on that dick.

"Uh, uh, I'm about cum baby."

"Come on, give me all that shit," he demanded.

"Here it come. Oh my God, I'm cuming!"

"Cum all on that fucking dick. Give me that shit. Now bend that ass over."

I leaned over the couch, Killa shoved every inch he had inside me. I didn't know what I was thinking trying to handle this dick again. Killa remove some of his dick then forced it back inside. He grabbed my hips and started digging deep in my pussy. I tried to run, but he slammed me back on it each time.

"Take this dick, it's your dick."

Hearing Killa say those words turned me on even more. He adjusted my ass to how he wanted it then slid his penis back inside me.

"That dick is so good, baby. Fuck me harder," I demanded.

Killa started to fuck me even harder and showing no mercy. I was screaming at the top of my lungs, and I was sure everyone in the house heard me. I didn't care, though, because this dick was good, and I didn't want this shit to end.

"Fuck, I'm about to nut." Killa groaned as he went crazy in this pussy. "Fuck!" He pulled out and nutted all over my ass then slapped his dick on my ass when he was done.

I put my clothes back on and sat down on the couch.'

"You about to be mad at me."

"Why? What you do, Killa."

"I made a mistake and nutted in you a little."

"What? Are you crazy?"

"My bad, it was a mistake. I tried to pull out, but that shit was too good."

I sucked my teeth. "Next time, we are using condoms."

Killa chuckled. "If it be a next time."

"What!" I said with an attitude.

"Chill, I was just playing with you."

"I know you told me we could leave in couple of days. Where are you taking me?"

"To my boss. Why, you scared?"

"Hell yeah, I am. I don't know what the hell he wants with me."

"Me either, but he told me not to kill you, so that's a good thing."

"What if he kills me, Killa?"

Killa looked at me as if he was thinking about what I said. "He's not. Stop tripping. If he wanted you dead, trust me, you would've been dead."

Killa grabbed his phone off the couch and stuck it in his back pocket. I forgot that I answered the phone for his wife. *I wonder if she's still on the phone?* I said to myself. We made our way upstairs and lay down. Star and Smoke must still be in the room getting it on because I hadn't heard nothing from them.

Me and Killa laid there with the television off and talked for a while. He told me his goals and how he wanted to turn his life around. The work he did now wasn't for him anymore, and he wanted to open a couple of businesses. I told him that he should do whatever he thought was best for him. Only he knew what was for him and what was not. Even though I didn't know what type of work he did, I was sure it wasn't good. I knew he was either a kidnapper, dope boy, or hit man. Honestly, I didn't care which one he was because I was falling for him regardless.

Killa

The next day

I didn't know what it was about Jada, but I was feeling her. Most would say I was moving too fast, and I agree. I hadn't even divorced my wife yet, and here I was falling for another woman. I was once told that you can't run from love, especially when it's meant to be. It wasn't not that I didn't want to try this with Jada. I just didn't want her caught up in the middle of me and Takira's shit. I probably should've thought about that before I laid the D on her ass.

I glanced over at Jada, she was still passed out. I got up and got dress then left with Smoke. We had to go collect some money from a nigga who owed Chief. We pulled up in the driveway and got out the car. I banged on the door, but I didn't get an answer.

"Go check around the back," I told Smoke, and he went to the backyard.

"Killa, I got that nigga," I heard him yell.

I ran to the back, and Smoke had him on the ground with his knees in his throat.

"Take that nigga inside the house," I demanded.

Smoke dragged him in the house by his collar.

"Where the fuck Chief money at, nigga?" Smoke asked.

"Fuck Chief. That nigga owe me."

Wham!

Smoke hit him upside the head with the pistol.

I heard bumping and moving upstairs. "Who else in the house?" I asked.

"Fuck you, nigga." I shot dude in his knee, and he screamed like a little bitch.

"Aw, shit, bruh. Why you shoot me, man?"

"Man, shut your bitch ass up," Smoke said.

I made my way upstairs and checked all the rooms. I found a girl upstairs in the closet hiding.

"Get your ass up." I aimed the gun at her.

"Please don't kill me, I'm pregnant," she said with her hands up. She came out the closet, and she looked like she was at least eight months pregnant. "Where the money at, and I won't kill you?"

"Inside the mattress. You have to flip it over, though," she said and pointed to the bed.

"Alright. Don't move, or I'm going to kill your ass."

I went under the mattress to grab the product, and this dumb ass girl took off running. I heard two gunshots ring out.

"You killed my baby mama? Fuck!" I heard the dude scream.

I grabbed all the money and made my way downstairs. As I step over the girl's body, blood poured from her head. I was going to let her live just because she was with child. I knew if she took off running, Smoke was going to off her. That's what her ass gets. She should've listened to me.

"I will handle him, Smoke," I said and handed him the bag of money.

Smoke grabbed the money, and I planted two bullets in dude's head. He fell to the floor on his face. Smoke grabbed the gasoline can and poured gasoline all over the house. He lit a piece of paper and dropped it then we made our way out the car and pulled off. I was glad that everything went smoothly. I had told Smoke time and time again to stop using guns without a silencer. For one, they draw to much attention. The only time you should use a gun without a silencer is if you're in complete danger, and you don't have time to put your silencer on.

After we left there, we made our way to Chief's office to drop the money off.

"I've been thinking about quitting," I told Smoke.

"What! Hell nah. Chief needs your ass, and nigga I do too."

"Yeah, I know, but I'm getting older. Plus, I might have a little one on the way, and I can't be living like this."

"I feel you on that. I'm not going to lie. I think about the same shit all the time. The money is so good, though, so it's hard for me to stop."

"True shit, but why not invest in something that will belong to you? We got enough money to get out of this shit for real," I said.

"I don't. I be spending like a motherfucker. Like I got Bill Gates money. One day, I'm going to leave that shit alone, though. I do need to do right for Lil Chaz."

"Damn right, you do because Laquisha ain't shit. I'm just being real."

"I know. My moms can't stand her ass. She said next time she sees her, she's going to give her an old school ass whooping."

We both burst out laughing because everybody knew Ms. Angie didn't play that shit.

"Just the two men I need to see," Chief said as soon as me and Smoke walked through the door.

Smoke threw the money down on his desk and took a seat, while I stayed standing.

"You're not going to take a seat, Killa?"

"Nah, I'm good."

Chief took a pull from his cigar and set it in the ashtray.

"Killa, did you think about my offer?"

"Honestly, I haven't."

"This a good opportunity for you."

"Yeah, I know, but I'm ready to get out this shit."

"I feel you on that, but I really need you on my team, Killa."

"I know, but—"

"But nothing. What if I let you run this empire?"

"I thought your son was doing that."

"Honestly, I don't trust my son like I trust you. You and Smoke know this operation like the back of your hands."

Smoke looked over at me, and I looked at Smoke. "Let me sleep on it."

"Alright, cool. Don't think too hard."

"Trust me, I won't."

Me and Smoke made our way out the office. I didn't know why Chief kept pressuring me be on his team. I knew I was one of his top hittas, but something wasn't sitting right with me. One minute his son, King, was supposes to run the company, and now it was me. That's some bullshit if you asked me. Now you don't trust your son all of a sudden? Just a week ago, the nigga was going to be running your empire, and you wanted me to work under him. Something was fishy about this shit, and I wasn't feeling it.

Chief already knew I wasn't working under no nigga I didn't know. I had been working under Chief for years, and I never heard him mention his son but once. So, what made him think I was about to take orders from some miscellaneous nigga I didn't know. I was too smart for that bullshit. I didn't trust easy when it came to niggas. For all I knew, he could be working with the boys or just a grimy ass nigga.

I would hate to have to kill Chief's son for crossing me. I already didn't like the nigga's demeanor; it just rubbed me the wrong way. It was like he had some type of animosity toward me or something. The vibe in the room was off, and I wasn't feeling that shit.

"You ever heard Chief mention anything about his son?" I asked Smoke as soon as we got in the car.

"Like once or twice, but I've never seen him. He told me he was engaged or some shit like that."

"I don't like that nigga."

"Why, what's up? You met him?"

"Yeah, last week he was in Chief's office, and he introduced me to him. I wasn't feeling his vibe. Chief told me that his son was going to take over while he ran his operation in Cali. Long story short, Chief said he needed me on the team, and I told him I wasn't working for his son, flat out. His son started talking shit, so I put his ass on his back."

"Damn! What Chief say?"

"You already know. Nothing, because he doesn't want these problems. Boss or not, I would off his ass too."

My phone rang, interrupting my conversation. It was my lawyer about my case with Takira. He had told me that Takira wasn't pressing charges, and he was going to get the case thrown out. He had pulled a couple of strings for me because he knew people in high places. Even though he charged me an extra $5,000.00, I didn't care. It was worth it. I didn't have time for no court shit anyway unless it was divorce court. I told him that I would have the money down there soon. He said okay, and we disconnected the call.

"How he going to offer you his empire after he already offered it to his son?"

"Exactly. I don't trust that shit."

"Me either. Whatever decision you make, bruh, I'm with you."

"Good looking out."

I dropped Smoke off to his car and made my way to my house. I hadn't been there in a couple days, and I needed to make sure everything was cool. Although I had an alarm on the house, there was no telling if Takira tried to fuck my house up or not. I pulled up to my house only to see Takira's car parked in the driveway. I hoped she was getting her shit, because if not, I was going to be pissed.

I walked in and called Takira's name, but she didn't answer. I walked upstairs into the bedroom only to see Takira laid out on the floor with an empty pill bottle lying next to her.

"Oh shit!" I said as I ran over to her. "Takira, baby wake up. Get up, please," I panicked.

I called 911 and tried to give her mouth to mouth. I start having flashback when my mother was on the floor half dead. Minutes later, the ambulance showed up, and I informed them that she was pregnant. They put Takira on the stretcher and rushed her to the ambulance. I got in my car and trailed behind the ambulance, praying that my baby was okay.

I can't lie. I felt bad for Takira, and I hated to see my wife like this. Even though we had our ups and downs, to see her lying there unconscious had me reliving my pass. I wasn't expecting to walk in and see her on the ground. I was hoping she was packing her shit and about to leave. I rushed into Christ hospital, but they wouldn't let me go to the back because they were working on her. All I could do was pray. I just wanted her and my baby to be okay. I waited in the waiting room for the doctor to come out. After about an hour, the doctor finally came out.

"Family for Takira Hutchins."

I walked over to the doctor.

"Hi, are you her husband?"

"Yes."

"Hi, I'm Dr. Dubai. I have some good news for you. Takira and the baby are both fine. Thank God you got there when you did. Do you know if Takira has any mental issues?"

"No, she doesn't. Why you say that?"

"Because she tried to kill herself. Do you know why she would do something like this?"

"Yeah, probably because we are going through a divorce. She has been really depressed about it."

"That will do it. Well you're more than welcome to go back and see her if you want. She's in room 217."

"Okay, thank you." I rushed down to the room.

Soon as I walked in, I kissed Takira's stomach and held her hand. She was still out like a light. I prayed as I held her hands in mine, and I felt her hand move.

"Deron," she said in a low tone.

"What's up, baby?"

"I love you so much."

"I love…" I hesitated because the truth is, I wasn't in love with Takira anymore. Don't get me wrong, I love her though. That shit doesn't just leave overnight. "I love you to," I replied seconds later.

A smile crept across her face.

I sat there with Takira all night until the next morning.

Next morning

"Good morning, Mrs. Hutchins, how are you feeling?" the doctor asked, waking both of us up.

"I feel a little better."

"That's good. We are releasing you today, but I need for you to get plenty of rest. Meaning you will be on bed rest for the next couple of days or so."

"Okay, thank you."

"You're welcome. I'm going to have the nurse come in here and check your vitals. Then, after that, she will do another sonogram to make sure the baby is okay."

"Okay."

"Any questions?" Dr. Dubai asked.

"No," Takira stated.

"Yes, I have a question. How many months is she?"

"From the looks of it about ten weeks. That's about two and a half months, but that's just an estimate. She would need to see her doctor for her exact date."

"Okay, thank you."

"You're welcome. You guys have a good day. Remember, Mrs. Hutchins to get plenty of rest. Oh, and drink plenty of fluids."

"Okay."

The doctor walked out, and the nurse came in. She took Takira's vitals then we went to get her sonogram. I was happy to see my baby on the screen; it melted my heart. Just to know that might be something connect to my blood line had me smiling from ear to ear. After we were done, the nurse discharged her, and we made our way home.

When we got home, I carried Takira to the bed and put on her pajamas. I turned on the TV and lay next to her. Takira laid her head on my chest and wrapped her arm around me. I wasn't feeling it, honestly, but fuck it. I just wanted my baby to be cool.

Takiraed end up falling asleep hours later. I was still up thinking about Jada. I knew she was thinking about me because I could feel her energy. After about another hour, I fell asleep.

Takira

I woke up in the middle of the night, and I was happy to see Deron lying next to me. I missed my husband so much. The day I took all them pills, I did it on purpose. I was staring out the window when I saw Deron pull up, so I ran into the bathroom and took the rest of the pills that were in the bottle then lay on the floor. When Deron came in, I was still conscious, but I felt my body shutting down. I knew before the pills did any damage, Deron would get me to the hospital.

When I got to the hospital, I remember them pumping my stomach, and the rest is a blur. Some people would say I'm dumb and desperate, but the truth is, I am. I would do whatever it took to get my husband back. Hearing him having sex with another woman on the phone broke my heart. I wanted to kill him and that bitch, but I couldn't be mad because I hurt him first. I was going to make sure he didn't see that bitch again.

I didn't know who he was fucking, but I had a feeling it was that bitch, Jada. I will make her life miserable if I find out it's her. I lay there and stared at my husband as I rubbed his chest. I then kissed his neck and made way down to his soft dick.

"What you doing? You supposed to be resting." Deron pushed me away.

"Come on, let me suck it."

I snatched Deron's dick through the slit of his boxers and stuff it into my mouth until it began to grow. When it was hard like I wanted it, I began to suck it.

"Fuck!" Deron said as I pleased him.

"Umm this dick tastes good," I said as I drowned his dick in my saliva.

Deron grabbed the back of my head and pushed his dick all the way down my throat. I bob my head up and down as I deep throated every inch.

"Damn, suck that dick," Deron growled.

I started to bob my head even faster and suck it at the same time.

"Fuck!" Deron groaned as he nutted in my mouth.

I swallowed every drop then climb on his dick and slid down. It felt so good to have him inside of me. I rode him slowly then bounced on his dick. The whole time, Deron's eyes were closed, and I couldn't help but think he was thinking about Jada or whoever he fucked. Usually, Deron would look at me while he made love to me. I kissed him, but he didn't kiss me back. I could feel his dick going soft, so I got up and sucked his dick again until it got back hard. I then glided my pussy back down on his dick. I rode him like I was on a wild bull.

"I'm about to cum, Deron. Umm shit," I yelled as my pussy muscles gripped his penis.

"Me too," Deron replied then released his warm nut inside of me.

I lay down on the bed, and Deron got a washcloth to wipe me off. I then grabbed my phone and turned the recording off before laid it down. Yep, that's right. I was recording everything. If that bitch, Jada, or any other bitch thought they going to get my husband, they had another thing coming. I would always be ten steps ahead of any hoe who tried to get my husband.

After Deron wiped me off, I lay there with a smile on my face.

The next morning

I felt Deron get up and start getting dressed.

"Where are you going?"

"I have some business to handle."

"Oh. With who, that bitch?"

"Man, don't start that shit, Kira."

"You fucked her, Deron?"

"Fucked who?"

"You know who! Jada?"

"Look, I don't have to answer to you."

"What you mean? You still my husband. Did you forget?"

"If I did fuck her, it's none of your damn business."

"I already know you did because you made a mistake and answered my damn call. I swear when I see that bitch, I'm beating her ass."

"If you know I fucked her then why you asking? And you're not going to do shit as long as my baby in your stomach."

I rolled my eyes.

"Don't you supposed to be resting? Lay your ass down, and I will be by to check on you later."

Deron finished getting dressed and left.

Killa

"You ready?" I asked Jada as soon as I walked in.

"Do I look ready?" she said with an attitude.

"Damn, what's wrong with you?"

Jada put her shirt on and tried to walk out the door, but I grabbed her by her arm and closed the door.

"What's wrong with you?"

I knew something was wrong because I could see the irritation written all over her face.

Jada folded her arms across her chest. "Where were you last night?"

"Home."

"Oh, okay. I'm ready to go now."

"What is your problem? We aren't going nowhere until we talk about this."

Me and Jada weren't in a relationship, but I didn't want her to leave mad either. I did have feelings for her, so it was only right I find out what was wrong.

"You still love your wife, don't you?"

I dropped my head. "I mean, I still got love for her, but I'm not in love with her."

"Did you fuck her?"

"Who said I was with her?" I asked.

Jada gave me that look as if she knew I was lying.

"Don't play with me. Did you fuck her, Killa?"

"Yeah, I fucked her, but it was nothing. I thought about you the whole time. To be honest, I was sleep. She started sucking my dick, and I fell for that shit. I'm not going to lie; my dick went soft a couple of times because you were on my mind. The only reason I stayed is because I was at the hospital with her after she tried to kill herself."

"Fuck you, Killa. You just like these other niggas. I don't know why I fell for your dumb ass anyway. I can't blame nobody but myself, though."

I walked closer to Jada, and she backed up. Her back was against the door.

"I don't know what type of nigga you think I am, but you better watch that fuck you word. One more thing. Don't ever compare me to another nigga. Do I make myself clear?"

Jada nodded. "Can we leave now?" she asked with an attitude.

I opened the door, and she stormed out. I shook my head because if it wasn't one thing it was another. Between her and Takira, a nigga was about to go crazy. I was really feeling Jada, and I wouldn't mind giving us a chance. Like I said before, though, I didn't want her caught up in my bullshit with Takira. Now, look, the shit was already causing problems. I had been thinking about Jada a lot these last couple of days. Everything about her was perfect. Her pretty face, her nice body, her sex was off the hook, and her smart-ass mouth kind of turned me on.

We put the girls in the van, and Smoke explained to Star that she couldn't get out when we arrived. The plan was to let Star go, but since we were running late, we didn't have time anyway. Me and Smoke got in the front seat, and I asked him to drive because I wasn't in the mood. All I kept thinking about was Jada being mad at me and what Chief was going to do to her. I didn't want anything to happen to her, and I'd be damned if something did.

"You good?" Smoke asked.

"I'm straight," I said and slumped in my seat. "I just got a lot of shit on my mind. Last night, Takira tried to kill herself. I found her on the floor passed out, and I had to call 911."

"Damn, is her and the baby okay?"

"Yeah, she's good, but the doctor said she needs to get plenty of rest. I'm salty that she is staying at my house, but I got to make sure my child is okay."

"Yeah, I feel that."

For the rest of the ride, I was silent. I kept thinking about Jada's fine ass. I didn't want to lose her, even though I didn't have her yet. I was planning to make her mine real soon. We pulled up to the warehouse, and Smoke opened the door then Jada got out. When Jada saw me standing there, she rolled her eyes at me.

"Ooh, Killa, what you do to my friend?" Star asked as she sat in the back of the van smoking her Kush.

"Nothing. She is tripping for no reason."

"No reason? Really, Killa? Ugh, just take me in the building so I can get this shit over with," Jada stated.

Smoke laughed. "Y'all two always into it," he said as he shut the van doors.

We walked Jada into the building and Chief came out of his office. Any building or warehouse he own, he had an office in it.

"Jada it's good to see you." Chief stated as he approached her.

"Wait, what are you doing here, Chief?"

"You know him?" I questioned, but Jada didn't reply. Instead, she started going off on Chief.

"Did you really have me fucking kidnapped?"

Chief laughed. "The answer would be yes."

"I bet your son put you up to this, didn't he? Where his punk ass at?"

Chief smiled. "Look, I need you to do one thing, and one thing only.

"I'm not doing shit for you."

Chief grabbed his gun off his side. "You're going to do it or I'm going to kill your ass."

"Hold up, Chief, you're tripping," I stated as I stood in front of the gun.

Chief looked at me up and down.

"You don't need a gun. You see she's already scared," I explained. "Plus, I thought you needed her alive."

"I'm not scared of his old cigar smoking ass with Elvis Presley pants on. Fuck him," Jada snapped.

Smoke burst out laughing "Them pants you got on is some bullshit," he butted in.

"I think you better watch your mouth," Chief said to Jada as he put his gun back in his holster. Tell your father he got thirty days to give me one point five million or I'm killing you and him. If he refuses to give me the money, you as good as dead. Oh, and don't try to hide because I got hittas everywhere. I bet you they smoke you like I do my cigars. Now try me, lil bitch." Chief adjusted his tie and walked away.

"Fuck you! You dirty motherfucker. My father not giving you shit. My father will kill your ass. That's why you didn't approach him. Old bastard."

Chief turned around and looked at Jada then blew her kiss. "See you in thirty days." He gave an evil laugh and walked away.

"Get the fuck off me!" Jada snatched away from me and made her way out the door.

Smoke opened the van door, and Jada got in.

"Girl, what happen?" I heard Star say right before Smoke shut the door.

We drove them to Jada's house where we let them go free. I tried to talk to Jada, but she walked in the house and shut the door. Although I had feelings for her, I wasn't about to chase anyone.

"Ahy, tell your friend to stop tripping and call me when she gets a chance. I already put my number in her phone." I handed Star both of their phones.

"Alright, you know she's stubborn," Star replied.

"Yeah, I see that."

I got in the van so Smoke and Star could finish they conversation. My phone vibrated in my pocket, and I saw that it was Takira.

"What the fuck she want?" I said under my breath.

I didn't answer her call because I was on my way home anyway. I was just waiting for Smoke to drop me back off at my car.

Takira

"Bitch, what? I know you didn't do no shit like that."

I laughed as I rubbed my stomach. "Yes, the fuck I did."

"Takira, you could've killed yourself and the baby. Did you think about that?"

"Nope, all I was thinking about was getting my husband back."

"What if you would've died from an overdose? Then another woman would be loving on your husband."

"No she won't because I will haunt that bitch and kill her ass. Bitch, I'm the real Casper."

We both bust out laughing.

"You know if Killa finds out you planned this, he's going to kill your ass. You know he hates sneaky shit. Not to mention the video you made without him knowing."

"Well, the video is just evidence for when I find out who he's fucking. I swear I think it's that bitch Jada."

"Well, don't jump to conclusions. Make sure you have all your proof before you go doing stupid shit."

"Okay, Princess. I'm going to call you back later."

"Alright."

Princess was right; I needed to make sure Jada was the person he was sleeping with. I was sure it was her, though, but who knows? After I hung up with Princess, I called Deron again. I had been calling him all day but no answer. I bet he was with whoever he was fucking the other day. I screamed at the top of my lungs because I was frustrated. The thought of another woman pleasing my man made me sick to my damn stomach. Long as I'm alive, the only woman that's going to sleep with Deron Hutchins was me.

Smoke

After I dropped Killa off at his car, I made my way to Laquisha's house to check on my son. I hadn't seen Lil Chaz since the day we went to get the DNA test. When I pulled up, I saw Laquisha's raggedy ass Honda Accord outside. That let me know she was there. Before I could even reach the door, I heard Lil Chaz crying over the music. Laquisha was so damn ghetto that she had her door wide open. I walked in, and Lil Chaz was sitting on the floor crying with shit coming out his pamper.

"Lil Cane, where your mama at?" I asked Laquisha's five-year-old son.

He pointed upstairs. This was the shit that pissed me off. Why was a five-year-old downstairs with a one year old? Lil Cane was still a baby himself, but she had him watching my son. I went upstairs to see what the other kids were doing, and they were in the room playing the game with some nigga. He looked like he was at least twenty years old. What pissed me off was he had her daughter sitting on his slap. I snatched his ass up and hit him in the stomach. He fell to his knees.

"Don't you ever in your life let a lil girl sit your lap with only her panties on. I will fuck you up. Now get the fuck out." I tossed his ass down the stairs, not giving a fuck if I broke every bone in his body.

I told the kids to keep playing the game and shut the room door. I walked into Laquisha's room, I'll be damn if she wasn't in there giving some nigga head.

"Bitch, are you fucking crazy?" I grabbed Laquisha by her hair and pulled her up off her knees.

"Smoke, get the fuck off me," she yelled as she tried to get me off her hair.

The dude jumped up and pulled his pants up.

"Damn, nigga, you on some cock blocking shit. Who is this dude, your baby daddy or something?" he asked as he buttoned his pants.

"Nah, nigga, my name is Satan. Welcome to hell, bitch ass nigga."

I wanted to shoot his ass between his eyes. The only thing that stopped me was the kids in the other room. Even though those kids weren't mine, I still cared about they bad ass. I let Laquisha's hair go and pushed her to the floor. Then I walked over to dude and smacked him like the bitch he was. He stumbled back and fell on the bed. I pulled my gun out then put it in his face.

"Nigga, you lucky my son downstairs, or I would kill your ass right here. Nigga, if you want your dick sucked, don't do that shit while my fucking son is here."

"Smoke, stop. Get off him," Laquisha cried.

"Now don't let me catch your bitch ass around here again, or I'm going to kill your ass on sight. Do I make myself clear?" He nodded. "Nigga, I'm a grown ass man. You say yes sir," I demanded.

"Yes sir."

Just like I thought, this nigga was a bitch.

I don't give fuck who the nigga is. There's no way in hell I would say yes sir to another man unless it's my elders.

"That's right, respect your elders, bitch ass nigga. Now get the fuck out before I light your ass up."

Dude wasted no time running out the door. I turned around and smacked fire out of Laquisha. I wasn't mad because she was sucking this nigga's dick. I was pissed because she was up there sucking dick while my baby was screaming at the top of his lungs. She didn't even think to check on our damn son. That shit had me pissed the fuck off. Not only that, but she was bringing random men in her house. Did she forget she had little girls? Kids are molested every day, and her as was bringing random niggas in her house. I didn't like that shit at all. What made me mad was her daughter sitting on a man's lap. I honestly wanted to break his damn neck.

"This the bull shit you do, Laquisha, huh? Sucking a nigga's dick while your kids are unattended?"

"It's my fucking mouth, and I can do whatever. If I want to suck a nigga's dick, I can. You just mad because it's wasn't your dick that was in my mouth." She rolled her neck with her arms folded across her chest.

I smacked the shit out of Laquisha, and she stumbled back a few steps.

"Bitch, who the fuck you talking to? You better watch your mouth. That's the reason I'm getting my son tested now because you nasty as fuck."

Laquisha stood there holding her right cheek as tears ran down her face. "I hate you Smoke!" She picked up the lamp off the floor and threw it at me.

I dodged it, and the lamp broke on the wall.

"If that lamp would've hit me, I would've fucked your ass up," I said as I stood in front of her.

"Fuck you!"

I slammed her into the wall. I knew the impact hurt from the way she frowned.

"I'm going to tell you this shit one time, and one time only. If you ever leave my son down there crying with shit on him again, I will slice your throat. Shouldn't no man come before none of these kids but God. That's why you will never be shit, you stupid bitch. Matter of fact, I'm taking my son with me. My mama wants to see him anyway.

"No, don't take my son nowhere."

"If I do, what the fuck you going to do about it?" I pulled my gun out and pressed it to her temple. "I will kill your ass in the blink of an eye. I better not catch no more niggas in this house, or it's going to be a problem. You understand that shit?" I cocked my gun and

Laquisha nodded. "Now, go get my son ready and clean this nasty house up.

Laquisha went downstairs and did what I told her to do. I grabbed Lil Chaz car seat and made my way to the car. Laquisha was in the door with only her panties and bra on watching me pull off. I don't know what the hell I was thinking when I busted in her ass. That was the dumbest shit ever. Laquisha was so sexy, though, and she would make any man or woman want her.

After meeting Star, though, I found everything I need in a woman. She was crazy, funny, sexy, classy and the sex was off the fucking hook. Star was mine, and she didn't even know it. I'd be damned if I let her ass go. Star told me she wasn't ready for a relationship because the last dude hurt her badly, and I respected that to the fullest.

I had to work on myself anyway because I had too many problems. For one, I couldn't stay out the strip club, my baby mama was ratchet as fuck, and I didn't need Star clashing with Laquisha. Even though I knew Star could handle her own, Laquisha crazy as fuck. She didn't know how to stop when it came to drama and would keep going on and on.

After she found out I fucked her friend who was a stripper, she popped up at her house and busted all the window out of the girl's car, her mama's car, and her husband. She flattened her tires, busted her house windows out, and smacked her sister. Laquisha was beyond ratchet, and I was sick of her ass. I swear I will never stick my dick inside her pussy or mouth again.

Laquisha was one of them types who would get pregnant by looking at the dick. See, when I fucked Laquisha, I used a condom each time. The last time I fucked her, the condom broke, and I didn't know. I didn't realize it had broken until afterward. It was too late then because I had already nutted. I was salty as hell, honestly. I even prayed she didn't get pregnant, but, unfortunately, she did.

Jada

"Dad, why is Chief after you? Is this the reason you don't like King?" I asked as I paced the floor.

"Jada, this isn't nothing you need to worry about," my father said as he put his clothes in the washer.

"I don't need to worry about it? This man had me kidnapped and pulled a gun out on me.

"What? He pulled a gun on you?" My father stopped what he was doing and walked over to me.

"Did he hurt you?"

"No, he didn't. Plus, Killa wouldn't let him.

"Killa? Killa who?"

"His real name is Deron."

My father stared at me and got quiet. "Deron, how do you know him?"

"It's a long story, Daddy. I don't feel like explaining all that. I'm focused on why Chief is threatening to kill me and you over one point five million dollars."

"Look, I promise you have nothing to worry about, baby. I will handle Chief and whoever else needs to be handled. This is why I told you to stay away from King. I knew he wasn't shit, but you didn't want to listen."

"Okay, Daddy, you were right, and I was wrong. But you don't have to keep throwing it in my face."

"I'm not."

I talked to my father for a little while longer. Although I tried hard to get information about Chief, he still wouldn't tell me anything. All my father kept saying was don't worry. When we were done, I made my way home so I could get dressed. I was going out with Star tonight to celebrate her birthday.

When I got home, I went right to the shower. For the last couple of days, all I had been thinking about was Killa. He had been calling me, but I had yet to return one of his calls. I was still mad at him for fucking his wife. Although I knew it wasn't my place to be mad, I still was. I had feelings for Killa, and they ran deep.

When he admitted to having sex with his wife, I felt my heart crumble to pieces. The sad part is he wasn't even my man. I wanted him to be, though, but I didn't tell him that. I felt I was moving too fast because I still had love for King. Although I didn't plan to get back with King, I still had some feelings for him.

I got out the shower and dried off. When I was done, I brushed my teeth and walked into my room to get dressed.

"Oh my God, you scared the hell out of me. What are you doing here?" I asked, breathing heavily and holding my chest.

"Why haven't you been answering my calls, Jada?" King stood to his feet and walked over to me.

"You got some nerve questioning me. You know exactly why I haven't been answering your calls. Did you forget you cheated on me in our home? Not to mention you and your father had me kidnapped."

"What are you talking about? I didn't have you kidnapped, baby." King grabbed my hand, but I pulled away.

"Well, your father did, and I don't appreciate that shit. He even pulled a gun out on me."

"I swear I didn't know anything about that. I'm going to check his ass." King pressed his lips against mine, and I pushed him off me.

"Don't put your lips on me. I don't know where the fuck your mouth been."

"Stop acting like that. You know you miss me just as bad as I miss you. Stop trying to fight that shit. I messed up, and I know I did, but at least give a nigga a chance to make it up. I will do whatever it takes to make it right, baby."

"I heard those words before, King, and I don't want to hear it again. Get out my house, now."

King stared deep into my eyes, and I could see the hurt. I wanted to take him back so badly, but I couldn't do it. After what he did to me, I didn't think I could ever forgive him. Every time I look at him or heard his name, I had flashbacks of him fucking that bitch Takira. There was nothing he could say or do right now to change my mind. King had made his bed, and now he had to lie in it with that bitch. He should've thought about what he had before he decided to cheat.

"I'm going to leave, but I'm not giving up on us. I'm going to keep trying until I get my woman back. I don't care if the world is ending, I'm still going to die trying," King said and then left.

"I got to get my locks changed," I said to myself.

I looked out the window to make sure King was leaving and watched him get in his car and sit there for a while before he finally pulled off.

Once he was gone, I got dressed in my white fitted jeans with my white half shirt and black red bottom heels. I put my real hair up in a bun. My hair was long and straight. My father had Indian in his blood, so I had a nice grade of hair. I grabbed my black clutch out the closet then made my way out the door. Once I was in the car, I called Star to let her know I was on the way. She told me that she was already there and to call her when I pull up.

The entire drive, all I could think about was Killa's fine ass. It took all of me not to call him. Star had told me he put his number in my phone, and I wanted to call him so badly, but I was too stubborn to do so. I just couldn't get over the fact that he had sex with Takira again, especially after what the hell she did to him. She didn't deserve him, or any man, for that matter.

Twenty minutes later, I pulled up to Reminisce night club and searched for a parking spot. It was packed, so it took me a while. When I finally found somewhere to park, I called Star to let her know I was outside. I got out the car and Star met me at the door. It felt good to be out the house after being kidnapped for weeks. That was the worst experience of my life but the best experience also.

When I walk in the club, all eyes were on me. I even saw a couple of women roll their eyes at me. I didn't care, though, that let me know I still got it. I gave Star a hug and handed her the gift I bought her. After that, I took a seat at the table and poured some champagne.

"What's up, Jada?" Smoke said as he sat next to me.

"Hey, Smoke, I didn't know you were here!"

I scanned the room to make sure I didn't see Killa anywhere.

"Why wouldn't I be? It's my baby's birthday."

I smiled. "True."

"What's up with you and Killa?"

I rolled my eyes. "Nothing at all."

"You know my boy really likes you, right?"

"I can't tell. If he did, he wouldn't be still fucking his wife."

"Soon to be ex-wife," Smoke said and took a pull from his Kush. "I think y'all need to talk. At least give the man some closure. I know y'all wasn't in a committed relationship, but a blind man can see the love y'all have for each other."

Smoke was right. I did love the shit out of Killa's ugly, sexy ass.

"Okay, I will think about it."

"Don't think about it, do it." Smoke got up and walked away.

I glance over at Star, and she was on the dance floor getting it in. I got up and joined her. We were shaking our ass like we owned the place. All the men in the room had their eyes on us, and of course, all the woman rolled their eyes. We didn't care, though; we kept give they ass a show. Smoke came behind Star and started dancing with her. Star was twerking the shit out of Smoke, and I knew he was ready to fuck her freaky ass.

I hyped my best friend as she shook her ass like a stripper. Next thing I know, some bitch pushed Star, causing her to fall to the floor. I snatched the girl by her hair, but before I could hit her, Star took over. The music stopped in the club, and everyone was standing around looking.

"Bitch, don't you ever put your hands on me," Star said as she punched the girl repeatedly in her face.

Smoke grabbed Star and pulled her back.

"This what you do, Smoke?" the girl said with an attitude.

"Laquisha, gone with that bullshit, bruh."

"You just mad I got your baby daddy," Star stated.

"Bitch, you must not have him because he was just at my house getting his dick sucked last night."

"Oh, you were, Smoke?" Star pushed him with all her might.

"Star, that bitch is lying, baby! I haven't touched that nasty bitch in months."

"Boy, you were just fucking me when you picked Lil Chaz up. Did you tell her that?" She stood there with her hands on her hips, and I could see the lil grin on her face.

For some reason, I didn't believe this Laquisha chick. She looked like a lying project hoe, and I didn't trust a word she said.

Smoke picked Laquisha up by her neck, and I could tell she couldn't breathe.

"Bitch, I will kill you. Stop fucking playing with me."

"Bruh, put her down," some dude said.

"Nah, Dame, fuck that. I'm sick of this ratchet bitch. I'm about to kill her ass."

Dame finally got Smoke off Laquisha. She was holding her throat and breathing heavily.

"I swear I got something for you, Smoke."

"Bitch, get any niggas, and I will fuck you and them up. You already know what the fuck I be on. My name rings bells in Cincinnati, and you know that."

After Laquisha stormed out the club, Smoke went over to Star and tried to explain himself, but Star didn't want to hear it. She tried to walk away, but Smoke grabbed her ass up. Star was crying, and that was something she rarely did. That's how I knew she loved Smoke without a doubt. I walk over to them so I could talk to Star. She was going off on Smoke, and he was still trying to explain himself. They both were drunk, and the shit was getting nowhere.

"Smoke, let me talk to her for a minute." I interrupted.

"You no good ass nigga. I'm done with you!" Star shouted.

"You aren't done with shit. You in this shit forever."

"I bet you I'm not. Matter of fact, I'm going to get me some new dick soon as I leave here," Star shouted.

"What the fuck you say to me, Star?" Smoke rushed over to Star, but before he could get to her, Dame caught him.

"I will break your fucking jaw! Let me find out any man been in that pussy, and I'm killing you and him."

I pulled Star by her arm out the club. She was still going off and talking shit while I was trying to save her from getting fuck up by Smoke. I could tell from the rage in his eyes that he wasn't playing with her. They were in love, and I could tell.

I had never in my life seen Star act like that over any man except her ex-husband. Star was with her ex for four years and married a couple of months. She divorced him after she found out he had got some girl pregnant. Come to find out, the baby wasn't even his. For years he begged for her back, but Star refused to give him another chance. Although the baby came back not his, Star said he still cheated, and she couldn't forgive him for that.

Star took marriage seriously. She felt like everything he said to her was a lie. The sad part was that Star wasn't going to marry him, but she ended up pregnant. She wanted a family with her baby and husband. Two months after Star got married, she had a miscarriage. Star was so depressed that she wasn't even washing her ass or doing her hair. Plenty of times I had to go over there and help her out. Her husband was so busy working that he didn't have the time to check on her, which was a sorry ass excuse to me. I mean, he had the time to fuck these hoes but not the time to take care of his wife.

When Star did finally came out of her depressed mode, she started notice that her husband had been out late and working more hours. I guess he thought that because Star was depressed, she wouldn't notice the changes, but she did.

One night, Star called me and told me to get dressed. I didn't question why or anything. I was ready for whatever. I knew we were going to do something we didn't have any business doing because it was 3 a.m.

Star picked me up and told me that someone had called her and said they saw her husband's car in North college hill on Cedar Ave. Sure enough, when we pulled up, her husband's Lexus was parked in the drive way. Star's temper was so bad that instead of knocking on the door, she threw a brick through the house window and climbed in. Sure, enough, her husband was in there fucking some dirty ass Dennis Rodman looking bitch. To make a long story short, let's just say me and Star beat the shit out the girl and him. We both went to jail for assault and breaking and entering. My dad bailed us both out the next morning.

"I hate that nigga!" Star shouted soon as she got out the door.

I could smell the liquor on her breath, which let me know she was under the influence.

"You don't mean that. You just mad right now."

"So, what? He thinks I'm playing about getting some new dick, but I'm so serious."

I laughed because Star was drunk as fuck and talking out the side of neck. "Girl, bye, that nigga will kill you."

"I don't care. He wants to fuck his ratchet baby mama, then I can fuck somebody too."

"You really believe he fucked her or let her suck his dick? I don't think he did. She looks like a sneaky ass little thot."

"Yeah, his little thot."

I chuckled. "Let me get you home because you are tripping heavy."

"Right, because I'm not riding back with his ass. I knew I should've drove my car," Star shouted as she opened my car door.

"I got her, Jada, don't worry about it." Smoke came out of nowhere and threw Jada over his shoulder.

"Put me down, you no good ass nigga," Star said as she kicked and punched.

I watched Smoke walk over to his car and put her in the front seat. He hopped in, and they pulled off. I swear, if I didn't know them, I would think they were married. They acted like they had been together for years.

I got in my car then made my way home. It had been a long night, and I couldn't wait to see my bed.

Smoke

I didn't know what had gotten into Star, but she was tripping hard. Star knew the situation with me and Laquisha, and I was mad because she let her dumb ass get in her head. I hadn't touched Laquisha's ass in a while, and I wasn't planning to either. I really loved Star's ass, and I didn't blame her for beating Laquisha's ass; she deserved that shit. She had no business pushing Star to the floor on some jealous shit.

That's the shit I hated about Quisha. She was petty as hell. If shit didn't go her way, she started acting a fool. How she mad because I had a woman, but I had just caught her sucking dick. This wasn't the first time I had caught her ass with another nigga. The other nigga didn't live to tell the story.

I can't lie, I had love for Quisha, but I was never in love with her. She just had some good ass head. The type of head that will drive a nigga crazy. The type of head that when you think about it, you start beating your manhood to death. Laquisha's mouth was dangerous, and she would drive any man crazy. I was cool on her, though. The only thing I was worried about was my son. I couldn't wait until those results came back.

Although I wanted Lil Chaz to be my son, I didn't want to deal with her ass for eighteen years. If Lil Chaz did come back mine, I was getting custody of him without a doubt. Laquisha would put up a fight, but I'd be damned if she raised my son the wrong way. The shit she does was unacceptable. Any real man would get their child out of that ratchet ass situation. I'd be damned if my son grew up around the bullshit that Laquisha be on. I knew I was deep in the streets, but when it came to my son, I made sure he didn't witness no street shit.

"What's your problem?" I asked Star as we cruised down I-75.

She smacked her lips. "You my problem."

"Solve that shit then. I didn't do anything wrong to you, Star. I don't know why you are letting Laquisha's ratchet ass get in your head. I already told you the type of person she is."

"Why would she say she sucked your dick, Smoke? Not only that, she said she fucked you the other night."

"Because she wants me. Can't you see that shit? Look, Star, I know we're not official, but I wouldn't disrespect you, especially not for her."

Star folded her arms across her chest. "Yeah, whatever. Take me home."

I pulled over to the side of the highway and turned on my hazards. "Look, I'm not about to play these games with you. Either you down for me, or you're not."

Star sat quietly looking out the window. I could tell she was drunk and high because her eyes were low as hell. I turned her face toward me.

"Look, Star, I'm going to keep it real with you. I love you, and I want to be with you. You can't let these hoes lie to you because they jealous. I never thought I would be able to settle down, but I did with you. We haven't even made it official, and I'm claiming you. I just got one question. Is your riding with me or not?"

I could see tears forming in Star's eyes, which let me know I had touched her heart. She nodded.

"I want to hear you say it, Star."

"I'm riding with you, baby," she stated.

I press my lips against hers and our tongues began to wrestle. I slid her dress up and her panties down then rubbed her clit until her pussy was dripping wet. Star gyrated on my finger as I slid them in and out of her moist pussy.

"Umm."

I pulled her right breast out and began to suck on her hard nipple while I fingered her. When I was done, Star pulled my dick out through my zipper. She leaned over in her seat and started sucking my dick like tomorrow was her last day on earth.

"Suck that dick, baby," I demanded as I palmed the back of her head.

I put my hand behind her and played with that pussy while she sucked me up. Laquisha's head was good, but she had nothing on Star. The way she sucked that dick had me beyond ready to make love to her ass. I was ready to pop twins inside that mouth and pussy.

Star reached over and leaned my seat back. She then climbed on top of me and inserted my long, thick pole inside of her, causing her to gasp for air. Once my dick was all the way in, Star rode that dick like it belong to her, and I was loving that shit. I smacked her ass, causing that shit jiggle.

"I'm about cum, Smoke," Star yelled as she rode it even faster.

"Come on, baby." I gripped her hips as she went crazy on my dick.

"I'm about to cum, Smoke! I love you, baby."

"I love you too," I said as I pumped deep into her from the bottom. I could feel my nut building up. "Fuck, I'm about to bust." Star hopped off my dick then jacked me until she caught every drip in her mouth. "Damn, that shit was was good as hell. Will you marry me?"

We both burst out laughing.

I push my dick back down in my pants then pulled off.

"See, that's why they call Cincinnati the Nasty Nati. Some nasty shit be going on in this city."

We chuckled.

I pulled up to my house instead of Star's house since I decided to let her stay with me for the night. When we got in, we went right to the bed. Before I could even get my clothes off, Star was passed out. I took off her clothes, leaving only her bra and panties on. After I covered her up, I lay down.

The next morning

I woke up to the smell of breakfast. My stomach was growling like a motherfucker, and I couldn't wait to eat. I thought I was going to have Star as my breakfast, but she was already out the bed.

"Hey, babe." She greeted me with a kiss, wearing nothing but her panties and bra.

"What's up?" I took a seat at the island.

"Nothing. I made you some breakfast."

Star scrape the eggs on to the plate along with some bacon, hash browns, and biscuits. She then set my plate down in front of me and my orange juice on the side.

"Thank you."

"You're welcome. Oh, UPS delivered some certified mail today," she said and set the envelope in front of me.

After I said my grace, I glanced down at the envelope, and it was from the DNA center.

"Shit, these the DNA results I been waiting on."

"What are you waiting for? Open it," Star said as she stood beside me.

I grabbed the envelope off the table and opened it. My eyes bucked when I read the results.

"What does it say?" Star asked.

Star hoped that the baby was mine because she knew how much I loved lil Chaz, and I would hate to walk out his life. That lil boy had my heart.

I took a deep breath and prepared to deliver the news.

Jada

I sat at my kitchen table eating breakfast and waiting for the locksmith to change my locks. King had me fucked up if he thought he was about to come in my house whenever he was ready. That was exactly why I had been looking for somewhere to move. I didn't have time for the pop ups. I was trying to get over King, and he was not making things easy for me.

There was a knock on the door.

"That must be the locksmith," I said to myself.

I looked at the time, and it was 10:45 a.m. That was around the time the locksmith said they would be there. I grabbed the money off the table and opened the door.

I was shocked to see Killa.

"You can't call nobody?" Killa asked and invited himself into my house.

"Killa, what you want?" I asked and closed the door behind me.

"You."

I folded my arms across my chest. "Call your wife. She seems to satisfy you better."

Killa walked up on me, and I backed into the wall.

"Why you keep playing with me, Jada, like you don't want this shit. I know you feel the love we have for each other because I feel that shit to. I know you want me just as bad as I want you, Jada."

Killa was right. I wanted him bad. I couldn't resist his sexy ass even if I wanted to. My pussy was getting wet just looking at Killa. It was screaming his name so loud I was surprised he didn't hear it.

"Killa, I don't have time for your bullshit today. I'm no one's second best."

"I'm not trying to make you second. I'm trying to make you first in my life. I know this shit might sound crazy, but I love you, Jada. In that short amount of time we spent together, I fell madly in love with you. I promise if you be mine, I will make it worth your while. I'm not the type of nigga to chase no woman, but when I see something, I want, I got get it."

Those words melted my heart, and I could feel myself getting weak in the knees.

"You want this shit or not, Jada?"

"I do, but..."

"Say no more." Killa kissed me before I could get the rest of my words out, and I returned the favor.

The door unlocked, and in walked King. Killa instantly grabbed his gun off his side and aimed it.

"King, what are you doing here?"

"Nah, the question is, what the fuck is he doing here?" I swallowed my spit because I was scared as hell.

"Wait, hold the fuck up! This the King you was with? This the King who was fucking my wife? The King who might have her pregnant?" Killa laughed.

"Pregnant?" Me and King said at the same time.

Killa cocked his gun, and King grabbed his nine out his holster.

"You better kill me, pussy. Don't no nigga pull they gun on me and not die. The only reason I might let you live is because of your father, Chief."

"Nigga, fuck you." King cocked his gun.

"Stop, please!" I yelled as I stood in the middle.

"Jada, baby, move," Killa said and pushed me to the side.

"Baby? You fucking this nigga, Jada?" King questioned as his nostrils flared.

"Hell yeah, she is. That shit belongs to me, and there isn't shit you going to do about it, lame. If you or any other nigga touch her, I will kill your ass." Killa kissed me while still aiming his gun at King. "Isn't that right, baby?"

"Say no more." Killa kissed me before I could get the rest of my words out, and I returned the favor.

The door unlocked, and in walked King. Killa instantly grabbed his gun off his side and aimed it.

"King, what are you doing here?"

"Nah, the question is, what the fuck is he doing here?" I swallowed my spit because I was scared as hell.

"Wait, hold the fuck up! This the King you was with? This the King who was fucking my wife? The King who might have her pregnant?" Killa laughed.

"Pregnant?" Me and King said at the same time.

Killa cocked his gun, and King grabbed his nine out his holster.

"You better kill me, pussy. Don't no nigga pull they gun on me and not die. The only reason I might let you live is because of your father, Chief."

"Nigga, fuck you." King cocked his gun.

"Stop, please!" I yelled as I stood in the middle.

"Jada, baby, move," Killa said and pushed me to the side.

"Baby? You fucking this nigga, Jada?" King questioned as his nostrils flared.

"Hell yeah, she is. That shit belongs to me, and there isn't shit you going to do about it, lame. If you or any other nigga touch her, I will kill your ass." Killa kissed me while still aiming his gun at King. "Isn't that right, baby?"

I nodded, and next thing I knew, bullets started to fly.

"Oh my God!" I screamed as I covered my mouth.

I had never seen anyone get shot up before.

To be continued...

COMING SOON!!

MY MOTHER MARRIED MY Rapist
BASED ON A TRUE STORY

SHERRI MARIE

CPSIA information can be obtained
at www.ICGtesting.com
Printed in the USA
LVHW051757171220
674450LV00013B/1126